'An ambitious work in which Kemp aims to give voice to the voiceless. Fast-moving and sharply written.'

Guardian

'A thoroughly absorbing and pacy read. A fresh angle on gay life and on the oldest profession.' *Time Out*

'Astonishingly textured prose and wonderfully defined narrative voices. I recognised the characters immediately and wanted to follow them.' Joanne Harris

'An interestingly equivocal and quietly questioning debut.' *Financial Times*

'London itself, in its relentless indifference, is as powerful a presence here as the three gay men whose lives it absorbs.' *Times Literary Supplement*

'A thought-provoking enquiry into what changes in gay men's lives as the decades pass – and what doesn't. As the connections and reflections across the years reveal themselves, this is a book that will make you think – and make you feel.' Neil Bartlett

'By turns explicit and energetic, Kemp's forceful prose uncompromisingly draws the reader in.' *Metro*

'Every now and again a new voice appears, someone whose stories speak to us on many levels. This first novel by Jonathan Kemp is one of those books. I didn't want this excellent   *cene*

'Above all, this is a story about the power of feeling and the hope and beauty that can be found in even the darkest places.'   *Dissident Musings*

'Kemp's language is beautiful, his characters carefully drawn and the dialogue engaging. The narratives overlap and are all the more moving for their subtlety. A touching and engrossing read.'   *Attitude*

'What an amazing book. This is the best gay novel to be published in many years. It is literary fiction at its best.'
                                    Clayton Littlewood

'*London Triptych* might find itself nestled between other works of gay historical fiction on the bookshop shelves, but its central theme – freedom and the pursuit of it – is universal.'   *Hackney Citizen*

'There is a deceptively relaxed quality to Kemp's writing that is disarming, bewitching and, to be honest, more than a little sexy.'   *Polari*

'Kemp has achieved what few writers ever will: a work that stands alone as a heartbreaking love letter not only to a vast and fascinating place, but also to the lives within that serve as its beating heart.'   *gaydarnation*

See p.193 for an extract from *London Triptych*

GHOSTING

Also by Jonathan Kemp

London Triptych
Twentysix

JONATHAN
KEMP

GHOSTING

First published in 2015 by

Myriad Editions
59 Lansdowne Place
Brighton BN3 1FL

www.myriadeditions.com

1 3 5 7 9 10 8 6 4 2

A CIP catalogue record for this book
is available from the British Library

ISBN (pbk): 978-0-9562515-6-5
ISBN (ebk): 978-1-908434-07-4

Designed and typeset in Palatino
by Linda McQueen, London

Printed and bound in Sweden
by ScandBook AB

For my parents

Each moment we pass through is made up of the past, the present and the future – three disparate temporalities all vying for attention; coexisting in their disunity. Over time we are contoured by these forces, much as a landscape is shaped by the elements. A sudden slippage can cause us to tumble, like Alice, into another world, because sometimes other worlds are closer than we think. We carry them within us, constantly.

DAY ONE

IT'S JUST AFTER nine am on a bright July morning when she first sees her dead husband.

She's stepping out of a newsagent's on Warwick Avenue when there he is, walking towards her through the sparse morning shoppers, like a figure from a nightmare in the garb of an angel. Handsome as the sun; shoulders broad as daylight.

Her first thought is, *You're losing it again, Grace.*

Dark and unsteady, she makes her way to the St Saviour Church, to sit among the voiceless dead and light a tremulous cigarette. Inhaling the first sweetsharp lungful, she lets the slow tears come. She feels – well, to be honest she feels as if she has just seen a ghost. And she looks as if she has, too. The face bloodless, the eyes dull as a seagull's, the lips slightly parted. All sound is muffled, slowed down, as if she's underwater.

A man walks by with two large huskies, one of which lopes over to her and sits by her side, as if sensing her sorrow and keeping her company. The man calls out, 'Ludwig!' but the dog does not move until he walks over and grabs its collar. He looks at Grace and nods a good morning before dragging the dog away. Finishing the cigarette, she immediately lights another, transfixed by a fear that makes her feel strangely alive.

Eventually, she gets up from the bench and leaves the churchyard; starts to make her way back to the boat, still dazed and unsure what to think. She hasn't given Pete a passing thought in years, though he still visits her in dreams which leave her aroused and unsettled the following day. That period of her life is ancient history.

When she arrives back on the narrowboat, Gordon is still out, so she sits up on deck, her mind in freefall. Gazing up at the cloudless sky as if it might hold some answers, she watches a plane slowly unzip the blue, wishing she were on it, going somewhere else; anywhere in the world but here.

It had been Gordon's idea to sell up and buy the boat once they'd retired. From years of holidaying on narrowboats they knew it was a lifestyle they both enjoyed, and she had loved the slow meander, stopping off whenever somewhere took their fancy. After a year of travelling they'd acquired a permanent mooring in Little Venice, and it hadn't taken long before the old life, the old friendships in Manchester, had slowly petered out. Now, painfully, she feels the pinch of her life, its very narrowness. There is no one to whom she can turn. Fear closes its cold hand around her: the fear of being taken back there, to lie and stare at those arrogant hospital walls.

Day One

She can't shake the image of Pete from her mind. Memories drop like ripe fruit at her feet.

IT WASN'T EVEN him she'd fancied, at the time. It was his mate, Mike, she'd spotted first. Him she'd set her heart on.

They met at Blackpool Pleasure Beach. And just those two words were enough to make you want to go there. They even tasted good on the tongue when you said them: sugary-sweet, like a stick of rock. Grace and her best friend Ruth, on a day trip from Manchester, one Saturday in late May 1958. It was the first really warm and sunny day of the year, and they'd both just finished school for good, feeling ripe with the invincibility of youth, kidding themselves they knew it all; giddy with a new sense of freedom. Scared of the world and fascinated by it in equal measure. Boys were part of that fascination, and part of that fear. And it was sometimes hard to tell the difference.

They had only just arrived at the fairground, and were discussing which ride to go on first, when she spotted them: two RAF boys in blue serge, one with a black quiff glinting in the sun – like Elvis, she thought, with a swoon. He spotted them at about the same time and she saw him nudge his friend and say something. The boys walked over and introduced themselves. 'Elvis' was called Mike, and his mate with the dark blond quiff was Pete.

'Are you from around here?' Pete said.

'We're from Manchester. Just here for the day. But we've been here loads of times before. What about you?'

'We're based over at Weeton. Just here for the day too. Fancy showing us around?'

'All right.'

Pete did most of the talking, cracking jokes, asking questions; focusing all his attention on Grace, who was trying her best to engage Mike, though he seemed content to leave the talking to Pete. Ruth just stood there, hardly saying a word. She was always tongue-tied around boys, which annoyed Grace as it left her to do all the work. As they approached the Tunnel of Love, Grace asked Mike where he was from, but before he could answer Pete said, 'Here. Let's go on,' pulling her towards one of the boats. Her heart sank. She looked over her shoulder to see Mike and Ruth walking towards the boat behind. Then she looked at Pete and thought to herself, *Well, he's not bad-looking, Grace, don't be so miserable*. Besides, Mike had been so monosyllabic she thought at least she'd have a laugh with this one, and not be bored like so many times before.

And then, in the chill, spidery darkness, they kissed. She'd been kissed before but never had she felt this aroused. It seemed so right, his lips on hers, that by the time they'd come out the other side she was in love.

As they clunked through the wooden doors and out into the sunshine again, and the kissing ended, he said, 'Where'd you learn to kiss like that?'

'I was about to ask you the same thing,' she said, feeling the rush of a blush as a devilish smirk sneaked stubbornly on to her face. He laughed, setting her off, and they cried with fits of giggles till their stomachs ached.

'You might want to reapply your lipstick, sweetheart,' he said, smoothing a hand through his hair.

She took a handkerchief from her handbag and gave it a lick before wiping the lipstick from around her mouth. Handing it to him, she said, 'You'd best give *your* mouth a wipe, and all. You look like Coco the Clown.' Opening her compact, she redrew the red on her lips.

As they climbed out of the boat, she wondered if Ruth and Mike had kissed, before deciding with a fickleness that surprised her that she didn't care. Judging by the look on Ruth's face – no hasty reapplying of lipstick there – they hadn't. She looked bored. Pete lit two cigarettes and passed one to Grace. He suggested the Ferris wheel next, where they kissed some more. Every ride an opportunity to kiss. After several more, they went for a walk along the seafront. It was a hot, sunny day and the place was heaving with people, but, like in the song, they all disappeared from view. He told her he was the son of a rich farmer and she told him about visiting her uncle's farm in Fleetwood with a cousin, Pauline. How she'd loved the newly hatched chicks, little fluffs of yellow small enough to hold in your hand.

He laughed and said, 'I was only joking. He's not a farmer; he's an officer in the Royal Navy.'

And she wondered why he'd lied, why he'd felt the need to lie, but brushed the thought aside and said, 'My Dad was in the Navy during the war; he's a fireman.'

'I only joined the RAF because it was either that or prison.'

'Prison?'

'Me and some mates got caught trying to blow up a sweet machine on the side of an off-licence.'

'Why would you do that?'

'Dunno – for a laugh? And we thought there might be money in it.'

'You bloody idiots!'

'I know!'

And it had all been so easy. No anxieties about not being pretty enough, or funny enough. Or too funny. She didn't worry that she was talking too much, or too little. With other boys she always felt awkward but with him she didn't. They talked about everything and nothing and laughed a great deal.

He said, 'I was conceived in peace, and born in war, on the very day it was declared.'

She said, 'Is that your excuse?'

Late afternoon they dropped into a pub on the seafront, and, while Mike and Pete went to the bar to order drinks, Grace and Ruth went to the Ladies.

'So how are you two getting on?' Grace said, checking herself in the mirror.

'He doesn't say much,' Ruth replied. 'And don't you think those luminous socks he's got on are a bit common? Mummy and Daddy would have a seizure!'

Ruth's parents owned their own house, and acted – in the words of Grace's father – as if their shit didn't smell.

'Who cares what they think?' said Grace. 'As long as you like him.'

Ruth gave a laugh and said, 'I wish I could be as bold as you.'

'Well, I'm having a great time.'

'I noticed. Mike hasn't even tried to kiss me yet.' She forced a smile and ran her hands down her skirt.

'I can't get enough, I can't,' said Grace, trying not to sound as if she was bragging.

Returning to the boys, Grace said they'd have to be getting a train soon. They took one last walk along the emptying beach, one last kiss behind a beach hut. A sudden draught on her back announced he'd undone her dress, and she said, 'You can just zip that back up as quickly as you unzipped it!' The sun was setting and they soon realised they'd lost the others. Grace was supposed to be home by ten and it was nearly nine. They rushed to the train station, but there was no sign of Ruth, so she boarded the next train to Manchester. He asked for her address, promising to write.

She arrived home at half-past ten to a smack on the head from her irate father.

'Well, you won't be hearing from him again,' he said when she mentioned Pete. 'Them Raff boys are only out for what they can get.'

'Take no notice, Grace,' her mother said.

And he was wrong. Pete did write, asking if she'd like to meet him in Manchester the following weekend.

FROM THE neighbouring boat a woman appears, wearing a brown velour tracksuit and white plimsolls, her hair snow-white and tightly permed. It's Pam – or Spam as Gordon calls her on account of her ruddy complexion.

''Ow are yer, luv?' she says in broad, salty Scouse.

Grace isn't at all sure she could translate her thoughts and emotions into words, so she simply says, 'Not bad, how about you?'

'I'm OK, just running late. You look peaky.'

'I'm a bit tired. Didn't sleep well.'

'Oh, dear,' Pam says. 'Anything wrong?'

'No.'

'Well, take it easy, put your feet up. Anyway, gorra crack on. I'm late for the hairdresser's. Let's have coffee soon!' Pam throws a quick wave before dashing off.

Grace goes inside and starts making lunch, deciding that seeing Pete like that must have been some kind of hallucination. Just someone who looked like him; an uncanny resemblance, nothing more. Right after he died she would see his face everywhere, momentarily staring back from the body of a stranger. It was the same with Hannah, too: as if your need to see them alive was so strong that you temporarily possessed the power to transform other people into the desired object.

But why now? She has no feelings at all for him now. She doesn't even hate him any more.

Throughout lunch, she says nothing to Gordon about what she's seen. She can imagine his reaction if she told him. He'd probably have her locked up again. The truth is, she loved Pete more, despite everything, and she knows Gordon knows this. He's always been jealous: mentioning Pete's name would not be a smart move, let alone confessing she's seen his ghost. So she says nothing. Not much is said at all, in fact, as they eat, and she's grateful for that, even if it also saddens her that after all these years together it seems they may have finally run out of words. Their separate routines keep them apart most days, and their time together now is encrusted with small talk, or silence.

After washing the dishes, she sets off to spend the afternoon on the allotment, starting to feel a little bit lighter, a little bit brighter, enjoying the sun on her face; able, finally, to put it all out of her mind. But then there he is again, Pete's ghost, or double, or whatever it is, stepping off a bus on Blomfield Road. Once again the sight of him stops her dead in her tracks, rips her heart from its moorings, untethering her reason. As she watches him cross the road she feels the heavy drag of something awakening within her, some unruly thing that has been shackled for years in a dank, unvisited cell of her memory.

She walks over to the bus stop and sits, trying to blink away the blind vision of him. Right down to the particular shade of his dirty blond hair, it is Pete. All the reasoning she had used to explain away the first sighting disintegrates in the light of this second. A quick vertigo takes hold. *It can't be real. He can't be real.* And yet it has such a disturbing reality that she no longer knows what reality is. Unsure whether to laugh or cry, she does neither. She wants to run over and fling her arms around him; she also wants to run a million miles in the opposite direction. If it isn't a ghost, what is it? Who is he? Is she really losing her mind again? Dear God, not that. All the ghosts in the world before that.

Bandaged in sunlight, she stands up and makes her way to the allotment, and as she works the soil, all through the planting and the weeding and the digging, thoughts keep circling inside her skull like searchlights looking for something approaching meaning, something resembling sense. She tugs at the corners of unfolded memories. Fragments in silt, seeds pushing out blind roots. All afternoon she loses herself in the shadows of her shadowed life, digging up the past in thick, cool handfuls.

ON THEIR FIRST DATE, the weekend after Blackpool, he had turned up with a dark mark on his neck. He'd said it was oil, but when she rubbed it, it wasn't oil; it was a lovebite, an accusatory bloom of purple and yellow. 'The lads did it – to make you jealous,' he said, explaining how a few of them had held him down while one bit his neck. Unsure whether or not to believe him, she had sulked for a while, smarting from the jealousy, then shaken off the discomfort of it, not wanting to spoil their time together.

He would always walk her home and her parents were soon charmed by him, impressed by his father's MBE in a way that slightly embarrassed her. Even her cold father warmed to him eventually. And in the ten minutes of privacy once her parents went to bed – before her dad would begin banging on the bedroom floor for Pete to go – she was never left in any doubt that he adored her.

After six months of insisting Pete stay at the YMCA on the weekends he visited, her parents finally allowed him to sleep in the spare room; and as soon as her father's snoring began rattling the darkness he'd sneak across the landing and into her bed, and her heart would not be still. While she cherished the feel of his body against hers, fear kept her from doing any more than kissing. She knew good girls waited, propriety hindering desire.

The summer before she'd met Pete, she had gone camping one Saturday night on Saddleworth Moors with a boy called Ian. Told her parents she was staying at Ruth's. And that night, as they'd lain kissing in the dark, he had placed her hand on his erection and said, 'Look what you do to me.'

Removing it from his pyjamas, she had touched its soft, firm texture, the give and slide of the foreskin. Its difference from her own body was both startling and compelling. In the dark her sense of touch became acute, and when she tried to picture it there came unbidden the memory of her naked father. That Sunday morning when she'd run into her parents' room to tell them the dog had been sick on the kitchen floor, forgetting momentarily that she was forbidden from entering. At the time – she was no more than six – she had had no idea what they were doing, only the immediate terror of an apparent violence: her mother crying out and him on top of her, grunting and sweating. She stood there speechless a while before her mother spotted her. 'Get out, Grace!' she'd said, pulling a sheet over herself. 'Frank, get her out!' And so he climbed off and strode towards her and she bolted downstairs, the slam of their bedroom door ringing in her ears and the tears running down her face, and the shock of what she'd seen between his legs indelible. But thinking of her father naked while touching Ian had only served to kill her arousal. She'd pushed the vision out of her mind. When he'd guided her hand into action she'd felt uneasy, and ashamed. Yet also powerful as never before. And when he came it was like a secret, or a lesson: the sticky mystery of men.

AMONGST THE cabbages, amongst the cauliflowers, these voices of the dead invade her thoughts, chirruping like birds on the branches of her memory. She finds herself holding up a fistful of wormdark earth and smelling it, inhaling its mulchy odour, locked to the spot. She throws it away in quick disgust and stands up; pulls off her gloves and grabs her bag.

She heads to Parliament Hill to watch the city melt into a pool at her feet. The endless sky up here always makes her feel small enough for nothing to matter. Nobody knows what she lacks. Thoughts lift from their slumber on the bed of her mind. A laughing crocodile of blue-uniformed schoolgirls swallows her up, oblivious to the grief swelling inside her: enough to fill the whole world. The heath grass sparkles. She closes her eyes and faces the sun, watching the light dance through her eyelids in movements of yellow and red. She can feel the wind rush through her as if she isn't there.

Making her way back to the boat, she concentrates on the things she can see around her: here, a blue-framed window; here, three boys kicking a ball; there, pieces of dismantled furniture – a desk? – leaning against a wall, and there, taped to it, a sheet of white paper, three words scratched in blue ink: *Please take me*. By these means she stops herself from dropping into the pit that has appeared inside her head. And, to top it all, she saw one solitary, sorrowful magpie as she was leaving the allotment, and though not normally superstitious she keeps her eyes peeled for another all the way home, but in vain.

Gordon is up on deck, cleaning the windows, when she arrives back. She says a quick hello and goes inside to lie on the bed. She can hear his irritating whistle. It isn't even a full whistle, which might not be that bad;

it's more, she thinks, a kind of half-whistle; this little piping sound like the kettle's hiss before its full-throated warble. She places a pillow over her head. *They say that if you think you're going mad you can't really be going mad, don't they? Whereas the mad have no idea they're mad – that's what makes them mad.* She, at least, has some idea that there is madness in these thoughts. She knows this is different from before – from the other great unravelling which led to that chattering ward full of damaged women. Now, each moment is lucid and present. She feels shaken, awoken, alert to these fragments of her past pressing into her, or out of her, like some kind of reckoning.

She imagines saying to Gordon, 'I've just seen your nemesis,' and bursts out laughing. But laughing to herself, with her head under a pillow, only makes her feel madder than ever. *Maybe I should just let myself get locked away. Best place for me right now. Away from the world for a while. Lock me up, and throw away the bloody key.* Her thoughts stagger like drunkards between an uncertain present and a past she doesn't want to revisit.

ON HER SEVENTEENTH birthday, just over a year after Blackpool, during a walk in Wythenshawe Park, Pete had said, 'I hope one day we'll get married, Grace.' And she had smiled and said yes, she hoped so too. And of course she was over the moon for she loved the bones of him, hardly able to believe her luck. She was lost to a romance that seemed real enough, and the future appeared filled with such sun-drenched certainty that she had no reason to believe she would be anything but happy. No reason at all.

The following weekend he drove her to Portsmouth to meet his parents, and, as they pulled up outside that big white house with its long gravel drive and immaculate front lawn, it struck Grace that his parents would think he was marrying down.

It was a bit like meeting royalty, or movie stars. From what he'd told her about his father, Edward, she had expected a more ill-tempered man, but she found herself quite charmed by this older version of Pete: same height and build, same big green eyes; same sense of humour. He cracked a joke about expecting her to be wearing a shawl and clogs like something from Lowry. Yet despite their similarity (or perhaps because of it) she sensed a tension between the two men. They behaved like boxers sizing one another up before the first punch was thrown. She noticed how Edward put Pete down all the time, and as the weekend progressed she liked her future father-in-law less and less.

His mother, Iris, was just as he'd described: immaculately dressed and groomed, with a warm but not fully sincere way about her. When she complimented Grace on the dress she was wearing, she marvelled to hear that she'd made it herself, going to such enthusiastic lengths with her praise that Grace felt embarrassed.

She couldn't imagine getting close to either of them, which, as things turned out, proved to be the case. After Pete's death she would take the children to see them once a year (always without Gordon, the very idea of whom they couldn't entertain). But they remained strangers, and after Hannah's funeral she never saw them again, and hadn't even gone to their funerals.

They'd been engaged for just three weeks when Pete received a two-year posting to Aden. They had wanted to marry straight away so she could go with him, but her father had said they were too young and insisted they wait. If they still felt the same way about each other in two years then they could marry. She was furious with the decision, pleading with her mother to talk him round. They were, after all, the same age her parents had been. It wasn't fair.

It felt like some kind of endurance test, those two years apart. Never before had she experienced such lovesick absence of another: this pining, this ache. Bursting into tears whenever 'Only the Lonely' came on the radio. Their only contact was letters. He would write often – sometimes three letters a day – and she reread them as if they were texts requiring close study, trying to get near to him through his handwritten words on paper. He wrote long, detailed accounts of his days, and sent photographs she cherished.

And she would reply to each letter, eking out the slim co-ordinates of her own routines: the typing job, the boredom of home life... always ending with a declaration of love and a reiteration of how much she missed him.

One thing she left out of the letters was the affair she nearly had with a married man, about a year into their separation. His name was Denis Middleton, and he was one of the senior clerks at Refuge Assurance on Oxford Street. He was thirty-six, with black hair smudged white at the temples. He would single her out to do all his typing, sometimes asking her to stay late to finish an urgent letter, and pretty soon small gifts – a pair of stockings, or a lipstick – started to appear in her desk drawer. One night he asked if she'd like to go with him to see a film, and she said yes, she would. Rang her parents to say she was meeting Ruth after work. It felt illicit and she didn't exactly dislike it. After the film, they went for a drink, and he told her about his wife being involved in a car accident and left paralysed. 'I don't want you to think I'm an adulterer, I have Margaret's full consent,' he said.

She told him about Pete, showed him the engagement ring. 'I'm not exactly in a position to judge, now, am I?' she said.

He never once tried to kiss her, but after a couple of months of regular trips to the cinema or a restaurant he had asked if she would like to go away with him for a weekend to Harrogate. She wasn't entirely shocked, and was more than a little flattered, but, feeling out of her depth, she'd said no. After that, he didn't ask her out again; some other girl started doing his typing and the gifts stopped.

Thinking of it now, she feels a wave of regret, wishing she'd been more adventurous, trying to imagine a different outcome. Knowing it's futile. It doesn't matter; none of it matters now.

ALTHOUGH PETE'S parents had wanted them to marry in their church and make it a grand affair, offering to help out with the expense, they opted for a small one in her local church, St Martin's in Wythenshawe. On his side there had only been his parents and a couple of his uniformed friends, including Mike, who was best man, and who was still courting Ruth, the maid of honour. In addition to Grace's parents were their siblings, her father's brother and his wife, and her mother's six sisters with their husbands and children. The seven sisters gathered like a flock of strange birds, clucking over childhood grievances every time they got together. For bridesmaids she had three cousins, with whom she still keeps in touch, albeit intermittently.

The day comes back in all its blue August sunshine: the white of the roses in her bouquet; the lucky black cat mascot Ruth had given her; the horseshoe-shaped confetti in Pete's hair. His laughter chimes in her head like bells, the lightness of the day returning to lift her mood with its recollections of a joy long gone sour. Back then, for one glorious fraction of time, she had had no reason to be anything but happy. She'd found a man as charming as a prince and could finally leave home.

She'd come to hate living with her parents. It felt like a prolonged childhood, a place she'd outgrown. And she wanted sex. She wanted, desperately, to let her body grow; was curious and hungry to learn. Adulthood so far had been nothing but impatience and restraint. And the wedding night had been a revelation. She hadn't anticipated how much pleasure her body was capable of. For her, it made their love all the more complete. The proximity, the intimacy, the realm of the senses.

Yet, as she began the task of living with Pete, even though it was three years since they'd met, it soon became apparent she didn't really know him at all. Being away from him had made her long for him and love him all the more – but it had also kept his faults well hidden.

DAY TWO

SHE IS ON A PLANE, surrounded by babies, all screaming their throats raw as the plane lurches and dips. She tries to calm them, to quieten them, but each time the plane jolts their screams become louder, more piercingly desperate – unbearable. No other adults are on board, no cabin crew: only dozens of crying babies, strapped into the seats, with their red screwed-up faces and loud open mouths.

All except one.

The baby in her lap is soundless as a doll. Sleeping. Or dead. And when she looks down she sees it's Hannah. Her Hannah.

The plane drops again and this time it doesn't recover – no hand of God to break its fall – only a rapid, furious descent. Just as it's about to hit the ground Grace wakes up, tense and disorientated, drenched in sweat, clutching the mattress. She stares at the ceiling, breathless and dogged by sadness. She looks over at Gordon. He is snoring, dead to the world. The clock reads 6.15. She lets out a long, slow sigh, which turns into a cough bad enough to make her sit up. Pulling on her dressing gown, she creeps out of the room, and daylight bleaches the shadows as her vision wakes. Making her creaky way to the sink, she fills the kettle, and pretty soon she's sitting up on deck warming her hands on a cup of tea. The marina is quiet at this hour, no one else around; only the muted sounds of the waking city reach her. She lights the first cigarette of the day and watches a family of ducks glide by.

They say if you hit the ground you die, with dreams like that. Falling dreams.

Has anyone ever hit the ground and lived to tell the tale? she wonders. Stupid thoughts like that, before-breakfast thoughts.

In the cool morning air, she distracts herself by writing a list of all the groceries she'd failed to get yesterday on account of Pete's ghost appearing. The sound of Gordon rising breaks her thoughts and she goes inside to make another cup of tea.

'Good morning, love!' he says, giving her a peck on the cheek. 'Sleep well?'

She watches him slot two slices of bread into the toaster. Gordon is a morning person, chirpy and bright. She has vampire blood in her veins.

'I didn't, no,' she says. She recounts the dream, and he gives her a quick squeeze before taking the margarine from the fridge. When Hannah first died Gordon used to dream about her all the time. Every morning, over breakfast, he would sit and recount vivid dreams in which he spoke to her, and in which she always appeared happy and healthy. Grace looks at him, at his round red face and sandy moustache, his quick dark eyes, and wonders what would happen if she told him; if she shared with him what was going on in her mind. And if she did – if she could make those sentences take shape inside her throat, find words another person might understand – how would he respond?

He switches on the radio, saying, 'Cheer up, Grace!' and sits down to slurp and chomp his way through his tea and toast. She leaves him to it and goes for a shower, wondering when, if ever, thinking of the loss will stop tearing her apart.

THEY BEGAN MARRIED life in Thetford, where Pete had been posted, driving down on the evening of their wedding day, after a brief reception, and spending their wedding night there before setting off on honeymoon – a week on the Isle of Wight. A sudden, clearblue snapshot of their first home. The memory of pegging out their bedsheets for the first time and feeling as if she was pitching a flag on the summit of her happiness; declaring her joy to the world.

But, once the ring was on her finger, Pete changed. Like black to white.

He started to criticise things she did and said, raising his voice and calling her stupid. The first time he actually struck her she'd been out to a dance with her friend Carol. Grace loved the socialising that came with

Forces life, and every Friday since they'd arrived they'd gone dancing with friends at a ball in the Officers' Mess Hall. Pete made friends easily, and pretty soon she knew everybody. But a couple of months into the marriage he changed, getting drunk whenever they went out and picking fights with men he accused her of looking at, moody when they were alone. Then he stopped going, staying at home and drinking. Seeing no reason not to, she still went out. She loved to dance.

That evening she let an American airman walk her home. Pete slammed the door on her startled escort before slamming his fist into her face. He smelt of whisky and she could taste blood. He turned away and started pacing the room.

'Why did you make me do that?' he said.

'I didn't do anything!'

'You're not going there again. Ever. Understand?'

'I'll do what I bloody well like,' she said, feeling tears prickle but refusing to let them fall.

'No, you fucking won't or you'll get another of those.' He cuffed her across the side of her head.

'You're not me dad.'

'No. I'm your husband. And I won't stand for other men walking you home, do you hear me? How the bloody hell do you think it makes me look?'

'Well, *you* never take me out.'

He held up his hand to strike again. Then he paused. 'Cunt,' he spat, lowering his arm. As he left, the slam of the front door made her jump and burst into tears.

Thinking maybe he was going after the American, she ran to the window. Pete was pacing up and down, smoking a cigarette in quick furious drags, staring at the pavement as if searching for something. She dropped the curtain and walked over to the mirror above the fireplace to survey the damage. The lip was split, blood all down the chin. Her jaw ached. *Well, the apple didn't fall far from the tree, did it?* she thought. She knew all about his father's treatment of his mother; how as a boy he'd slept with a knife beneath his pillow, scared of his father's rage. She had listened to those stories and felt nothing but sympathy for that terrified little boy. Now all she felt was impossible anger. And the fear that he might do it again.

Her whole body tensed as he re-entered the house, but when she turned to face him he was sobbing like a child. He walked over and held her, begging forgiveness, promising never to strike her again. He said, 'I love you' over and over, trembling in her arms. She held him as if he would break. Numbly she received his kisses, which grew more and more passionate, till they were fucking right there on the floor. Nothing more was said of the bruise on her face; or the crack that had appeared in her heart.

And she never went dancing again.

AFTER HER SHOWER, she washes the breakfast crockery. Gordon has gone out somewhere; she doesn't know where. She goes into the bedroom to make the bed, but instead she lies down and pulls the duvet over her, to voyage in the dark.

IT WAS THREE MONTHS before he hit her again. Valentine's Day 1962, their first as husband and wife. She'd only found out a couple of days before that she was expecting, and had decided to wait to tell him. She'd wanted to fall pregnant for so long that it was hard to keep it a secret. But she did. She had shaved her pubic hair into the shape of a heart. Still in love with him, despite everything. Scared of him, a little, sometimes, but still in love. Still in thrall to those moments of tenderness and passion when their bodies locked in a single mission.

When he arrived home empty-handed, saying he'd forgotten what day it was, she pretended it didn't matter and gave him her card. Inside it, after her name, she had written +1, and as he opened it she watched his face, waiting for the smile that never came. Instead he went to the front door, opened it, and came back with a dozen red roses and a card.

'You could look more pleased about it,' she said, and went to serve the dinner, which they ate in silence until he said,

'I am pleased. Of course I'm pleased. I'm just worried how we'll afford it.'

'I'll get a job.'

'I've told you, I don't want you working.'

'Well, I'll take in sewing, then. We'll manage.'

Ghosting

By the end of the meal he'd slipped into a sullen, spiky silence, which, when she prodded it, flared up till he was pushing her against the wall and knocking his fist against her skull. Half an hour later, after his tears and apologies, they were sweeping the plates off the table in their haste to couple. And that became the pattern. A beating, then his remorse, followed by her forgiveness. Followed by sex. Over the next four years they became trapped in this crazy, predictable cycle. And if she'd thought starting a family would calm Pete down she was sorely mistaken; if anything, it made things worse. A year after Hannah came Paul, and she doted on them, giving them all the love she had to give. Whenever she asked Pete to help with the children he'd say, 'You wanted them; you take care of them. I work to keep them clothed and fed,' before storming out. He found reasons to stay away from home, coming in drunk and arguing, waking up the children, flying into violent rages that left her bruised inside and out. Her life took on a shape she could barely recognise. Treading on eggshells and dodging bullets.

She thought of leaving him many times, usually after a fight, full of rage and frustration and aching from his punches. But she had nowhere to go, and no money, nor any way of getting any, and no one to turn to. She would fall asleep resolving to leave in the morning, but when she woke up she'd always changed her mind. By then she was no longer angry; he would've apologised, saying she'd made him do it but begging for forgiveness, telling her how much he needed and loved her, promising to change. And she would forgive him, time and time again.

Yet with each blow her love for him diminished. She would say she loved him but she felt it less and less.

By the time she fell pregnant with Jason, they were living in Mid Glamorgan, and the violence had become more frequent, and Grace more adept at hiding the bruises. When she told him about the baby he insisted she get rid of it, but she wouldn't.

Four months into the pregnancy, Pete received a posting to Malaysia and suggested she stay behind until the child was born. It would be easier, he said. She moved back in with her parents in Manchester and the night before he left, in the heat of another row, he pushed her downstairs. Two broken ribs and a fractured left wrist... but at least she didn't lose the baby. She told her parents and the doctor she had fallen.

Fallen for the wrong man.

To be free of that, for a while at least, seemed like bliss. She was grateful for the respite from Pete's violence. His absence brought a calm to her life she cherished. Yet at the same time the countdown had begun – the countdown to that day when she would have to join him on the other side of the world, in a strange place where she knew no one but him. So, while she had loved being pregnant with Hannah and Paul, she hated being pregnant with Jason; each day he grew inside her brought her nearer to Pete.

The one time she tried telling her mother about the violence, her response was, 'There are things that go on between a husband and wife that are nobody else's business. Sometimes marriage is hard.'

THE SOUND OF the television announces Gordon's arrival, its volume loud enough to shatter her reverie. She pulls the duvet from her face and slowly hauls herself to the sore, cramped daylight at the other end of the boat, still caught in the cobwebs of another realm.

'How was the allotment?' Gordon says.

'I didn't go; went back to bed.'

She checks the clock on the wall. 12.36. The passage of time it marks means nothing to her. The outside world keeps track in a way the inner world refuses to. She feels jetlagged from navigating these two time zones.

'Are you ill?' he says.

'I just didn't feel too brilliant. I'm a bit better now.'

'I was hoping you'd have brought some veg back.'

After lunch, he leaves again and Grace goes into the bedroom and opens the wardrobe, taking out a cardboard box with the words 'Hannah's Things' written on the side. Most of Hannah's belongings went to charity shops: the records and the books that meant nothing to Grace; all of the clothes and shoes. But a few, carefully chosen items went into the box. Her Hannah shrine. An archive unopened all this time. Over a quarter of a century.

- Hannah's first lock of baby hair, a frail blonde tuft coiled inside a faded pink envelope with the words 'Hannah Rose' written on the front in green ink.
- Some of Hannah's favourite books: *The Water Babies*, *The Little Prince*, *The Secret Garden*, *Little House on the Prairie*.
- The first dress Grace had made for her when she was two.
- Three diaries and a journal from the last three years of her life.
- All her school reports and photographs.
- A series of drawings Hannah drew at the age of seven or eight that told the story of a princess who married a succession of princes, all of whom died a horrible death. Each picture depicted the various deaths: decapitation, falling from a tower, speared with arrows, trampled by horses, drowned, poisoned; the princess finally living Happily Ever After Alone.

Grace carries the box from the bedroom and sits in front of the dead eye of the television screen. She removes the diaries, which date from 1976 to 1978, covering the ages of thirteen and a half to sixteen, and the later journal, that were among Hannah's things when she died. Looking at them now, Grace conjures the stories they contain, which escape into the room like smoke to form the shape of a girl who tells as best she can the sum of her time here. Even the diaries themselves seem to map the trajectory of Hannah's descent, the first two covered in pink and blue floral patterns, each with a small gold lock and little matching boxes; the third grey; the journal a black, unlined exercise book, the entries random but nearly always dated.

She pictures the blonde beauty of Hannah aged eleven or twelve, and then the vision of her just before she left home for good, her hair dyed bright red and her face ghostly white, black eyes and purple lips, clothed head to toe in black. By that time, all Grace had wanted was for Hannah to like her again, enough to want to spend some time with her, to say 'I love you, Mum,' as she had when she was a child. Knowing that was never going to happen cut deep, with a finality that still wounds.

She opens one of the diaries to find, tucked inside, a batch of a dozen or so photographs of Hannah, a visual representation of her growth, from bonny blonde baby and pretty blue-eyed child to the last picture of her ever taken. It's a colour photo, though it could be black and white for all the colour it contains. Hannah is dressed in black, with black dyed hair all crimped and spiked; her face white panstick with black eyes and lips. It was taken during a holiday in Malta. Hannah hadn't wanted to go and it shows. Fifteen years old and all wound up with murderous contempt for a world she didn't understand, or which she'd measured and found wanting. By then she'd grown to hate having her picture taken, but Grace had insisted. It was almost as if she'd known that six months later Hannah would leave home for good; a year after that, she would be dead.

She puts the photographs back in the diary and closes it. She doesn't need or want to read these books again. Instead they read her, in memories of words scratched across some place deep inside, like graffiti on a prison wall. Without opening it, Grace knows that most of the pages in the 1978 diary are blank, representing those final months when Hannah was hardly ever at home. The last entry, on her sixteenth birthday, is the one word *Leave*. With a tightness in her chest, Grace wonders, again, for the millionth time, what made Hannah lock her out; what caused her to hide the agonies she was enduring. 'Why didn't you *tell* me?' she says to the girl sitting opposite her, who says nothing, of course. It breaks Grace's heart to recall how Hannah went from the happy girl she loved to the angry, damaged teenager she grew scared of, making herself harder and harder to love with each passing day, as she burrowed further away from everyone to a place where no one could reach her. By then, she'd become uncontrollable; there was no reasoning with her. Whenever anyone spoke to her she reacted like a scalded cat. What the hell were you supposed to do?

THEY'D ALWAYS JOKED that Hannah had nine lives, because of the many times they nearly lost her. Five months into the pregnancy Grace had started to bleed, and at the hospital the doctor had said, 'If you believe in God, start praying. That's the only thing will save this baby now.' She didn't believe in God – never had, beyond the habits of childhood prayer – yet in that noisy ward she said, 'Dear God, please let me keep this baby.'

It was a home birth, and when her waters broke the midwife noticed the fluid was green, a sure sign the baby wasn't alive. But she *was* alive, and kicking. Three weeks late but perfect.

Around the age of two, Hannah started throwing tantrums, holding her breath until her face went bright red. One time she went blue and stopped breathing altogether. Passed out cold. For a moment Grace had thought she was dead, scooping her up in her arms, screaming her name, until, with a cough, her small eyes opened and she pushed Grace away. It seems she was always pushing her away, all her life, one way or another.

When Hannah was three, on the day before they left Thetford for Glamorgan, during their last trip to the beach, she disappeared. And as they searched for her, calling her name, Grace was lost to a single unthinkable thought. The flood of relief when she was found unharmed, bawling to wake the dead... She'd been spotted by an old man walking his dog, who said he'd seen a large rock fall right next to where she had been playing in pools at the foot of a high cliff.

There were two near-deaths by water, the first not long after returning from Malaysia, during a day out in

Day Two

Tatton Park. Hannah had slipped and lost her footing while crossing a shallow brook, and the shock of falling into the water panicked her and she flailed around until Paul waded in and rescued her. The second time was a good few years later, when she was – what? Thirteen? And already lost to Grace by then. She'd stormed off in a mood after an argument, going out in the inflatable dinghy and drifting too far, caught in a current which carried her further and further out. That time she'd been saved by Jason, a strong swimmer even then.

But the last time, when she was nearly sixteen, just before she left home for good, was by far the worst. It was around nine pm on a Saturday night, and as usual Grace was alone in front of the television. Gordon was down at the snooker hall, Paul was out, and Jason had just gone to bed. Grace heard the back door opening and a flurry of whispered voices. When she reached the kitchen there was only Hannah, slumped in a chair, unconscious. She called her name, and shook her, pulled back eyelids to reveal bloodshattered pink. She slapped her across the cheek, but Hannah didn't stir. Unsure whether to call 999, Grace carried the girl into the lounge and laid her down on the settee. From the kitchen she fetched a cold cloth to soothe her hot brow, all the time saying her name. After ten minutes she phoned for an ambulance; but just as she was ending the call Hannah regained consciousness, storming out before the ambulance arrived, leaving Grace the embarrassment of explaining to the paramedics what had happened.

They'd handed her a leaflet about drugs which she still doesn't understand why she never read.

GRACE RECALLS the first time she'd read the diaries, on the anniversary of Hannah's death. A year in which, after the first few weeks, even mentioning Hannah's name had drawn a disapproving silence from Gordon and her two sons. They didn't seem to feel Hannah's death the way Grace did; or perhaps, to be fair, they dealt with it differently. For Grace, life had lost all colour and purpose. Something had been torn from her, and all she wanted to do for the remainder of her time alive was roar like a beast at slaughter. Her firstborn was dead, and she knew, in the form of a pain that would never lessen, that nothing could ever be real again.

When she had suggested they all visit Hannah's grave together to mark the anniversary, Gordon said, 'It's been a year now, Grace. We all need to forget, not keep remembering. Hannah's gone, and we need to move on. *You* need to move on.'

'But that's exactly why we should remember her – because she isn't here,' she replied.

'You go, if it means that much to you,' he said, 'but I'm not taking the day off work to visit a grave, it's morbid; and the boys will be at school.'

So she went alone.

It was a sunny October day, the sky bright and cloudless, the light bringing out the colours of the flowers she'd taken to put by the headstone. As she sat at the graveside, talking to her dead daughter, the loss, the terrible loss cut through her again, its dimensions so vertiginous she found herself clinging to the grass beside her for fear of falling off the planet, or else being left behind as it plummeted beneath her.

She'd fled back to the house, and, grabbing a roll of black bin bags from the drawer in the kitchen, she had gone up to Hannah's room, pausing at the door, hand on handle. Every day for the past year she had come in here and lain on the bed, or walked around touching Hannah's things. It had been kept just as it was when Hannah left: posters on the walls, the bed made. Now, she knew, it all had to go. She set to work emptying wardrobes and drawers, stuffing their contents into bin liners. Before long she'd unearthed the green canvas bag the police had given her. She had placed it at the top of the wardrobe immediately after they left, and then forgotten about it. She picked it up and tipped its contents on to the bed. A make-up bag, a purse... and the diaries.

As she read them that afternoon, Grace had discovered a secret account – a fragment – of her daughter's last four years: from the childish innocence of the early entries to the uncomfortable knowledge of Hannah's first sexual experiences; from the simplicity of '*Top of the Pops* was complete rubbish tonight' to the raw pain of 'Right now I just want to die'; from sending a birthday card to John Travolta, to her first taste of heroin.

She discovered that Hannah had been bullied at school by a girl called Jackie Kirby, and this knowledge threw so much light on her behaviour that it saddened Grace to think of it again now, to recall how sullen and withdrawn Hannah became. But, whenever Grace had asked what was wrong, she'd shrugged and walked away saying, 'Nothing. Just leave me alone.'

Hannah's saviour from Jackie's tyranny had been a new girl, Alicia, who had transferred from another school after being caught sniffing glue, and who'd appeared at the desk next to Hannah one day like an avenging angel, teaching her how to smoke and protecting her from the bullies. Grace recalled a well-spoken, well-mannered girl from Hale Barns, but the diaries told a different story. She was shocked to read about truancy and pot-smoking with Alicia and her older brother Mark.

The entry for New Year's Day 1978 read:

Bad Habits
> *Never on time*
> *Late being born*
> *Late ret. Libr. Bks.*
> *Late for sch.*
> *Smoking*
> *Drink*
> *Drugs*
> *Sex (?)*
> *Sour milk in tea*
> *Chocol. biscuits*

Day Two

Angry
Moany complain
Fighting
Materialistic

Next to this list were blue doodles of stern angular faces and something that looked like a jellyfish or perhaps a lampshade – Grace couldn't tell which – along with some shape resembling an iced bun with a cherry on top, or was it a volcano? It put her in mind of both. There were entries in which Hannah berated Grace: vicious attacks full of hatred and disdain, calling her stupid and pathetic.

To say it destroyed her to read all this would be an understatement. When Gordon came home from work that day he found her naked in the front garden, scraping at the dirt like a dog, digging as if wisdom, like most precious materials, must be ripped from the earth's entrails. She was cramming soil into her mouth as if there were nothing tastier. Lost to all reality but the mulch beneath her nails and the feral grit in her mouth.

Gordon managed to get her inside the house and call an ambulance. He wrapped her in a dressing gown and asked her what on earth she'd thought she was doing. She said nothing. She had still said nothing when the men arrived. She panicked at the sight of them and tried to bolt, but they wrestled her into a straitjacket and out to the ambulance. Gordon stayed in the house and signed the section papers. She screamed his name, screamed for release. She was driven to Parkside Hospital, its Victorian foreboding illuminated by the blue wash of a full moon, the clock tower a raised fist of masonry.

GRACE FEELS Gordon's arrival, rocking the boat as he steps heavily on to it; and then she hears him call hello. She quickly replaces the diaries and puts the box away.

After dinner, feeling cooped up, on the pretext of needing to buy cigarettes, she goes for a walk. 'I won't be long,' she says, but he makes no response, engrossed in the television – an assessment of Gordon Brown's first month in the office he'd always wanted, by the sound of it. She's grateful to escape its insistent drone.

The sky is a white, pink and blue parrot's wing. She passes some neighbours out on their deck and bids them good evening, making her way up on to the street. She walks for miles with no clear destination in mind, past pubs spilling over with people enjoying the weather; past houses filled with families. She is carrying Hannah's dead body in her arms, and she doesn't want to put it down but she doesn't want to carry it any further. She blinks back a tear, pausing to feel the weight of her exhaustion.

She loses herself in imagining never having been born at all. It isn't so much that she wants to end her life, but for the first time death presents itself to her now, in one clean moment, as such a clear solution that it doesn't even fill her with dread to think about it. She tries to imagine Hannah's last minutes, slipping away in a numb fog of opiates, like a drowner submitting to the clutch of the last breath; thinks of Pete's, wondering if she was in his final thoughts.

She watches buses pass, picturing herself jumping in front of one, wondering what force of courage or will it would take, and how it would feel in that split second of impact. Or perhaps she should fill her pockets with stones and walk into the canal? Or jump from a bridge and make a hole in the strong brown Thames? Procure some sleeping tablets and dream forever? For over an hour she walks, dazed by such thoughts. Eventually, overwhelmingly wearied, she finds a bench and sits down.

A man approaches and asks if he can sit next to her – an old man, in shabby attire with unkempt hair and a long white beard, bringing with him the scent of booze and tobacco and ancient sweat.

'You look like you could do with some company,' he says.

'Be my guest,' she says, thinking, *And you look like you could do with a bath*.

'And what brings you here, out of all star-flecked possibilities?' he says. The sky is a deep, vivid blue now the sun has set.

'I just don't want to go home,' she says.

'And I have no home to go to. What a pair we are.'

'What happened?' she asks, offering him a cigarette.

'What didn't happen? Five years ago I lost my wife, then my job, and then, finally, the will to live. Lost the house not long after. Been sleeping rough ever since.'

'I'm sorry. Did she die?'

'No. Walked out. Moved in with my best friend. They'd been at it for years.'

A police siren sounds in the distance, and in the silence that follows she says, 'I think my marriage is over, but I don't know where else I can go.'

'Beyond repair?'

'I don't know. Don't know how to know.'

'"Every bond is a bond to sorrow",' he says. 'James Joyce.'

'Grace Wellbeck,' she says, and he laughs and says,

'No, I was quoting James Joyce. He was a writer. My name's Patrick.' Shifting the cigarette to his left hand, he holds out his right and Grace enjoys the surprise of his skin's rough warmth. 'Patrick Dodgson,' he adds, 'Pleased to meet you.'

'Likewise,' she says.

'Where's your husband now?'

'Back at home; we live on a narrowboat.'

'Nice. Have you tried talking to him?'

'Yes, but it's impossible. He thinks I'm crazy.'

'And are you?'

'No, but I would say that, wouldn't I?' she says with a laugh.

'Maybe he's the mad one,' he says. 'Are any of us really in a position to judge?'

'The thing is, Patrick,' she says, watching a couple stroll past arm in arm, dressed in the moon's muted colours, 'I think I'm being haunted.'

'Aren't we all being haunted, one way or another?'

'I don't know about that, but I keep seeing the ghost of my first husband.'

'Ah.'

'Well, I say ghost, but I've never believed in ghosts. But I don't know how else to explain what I've seen.'

'A conundrum, to be sure,' he says, taking a nip from the bottle he's just removed from his jacket pocket. 'Care for some rum? I find it helps in times of doubt.'

She wipes the top of the bottle with the palm of her hand and takes a sip. 'Do you believe in ghosts?'

'I believe in the power of the human mind to conjure up all manner of delusions to soften the blow of existence,' he says.

'You think I'm deluded?'

'I didn't say that. I think if you see a ghost you should follow it; learn from it all you can. You may never see another. What is a ghost, after all, but a wound that's yet to heal?'

He leans forward suddenly, tipping his face up to the street-lamp's weak illumination, and asks her to guess his age. The beard and greying hair make it hard to determine. Between blinks the eyes are sharp and pale; the skin tight with lines and the lips are chapped. Before she can hazard a guess he says, 'I'm forty-two, though I'd bet money on it – had I any and were I a gambling man – that you thought I had a good ten years more.' He seems pleased with this, as if he has foxed her with some riddle.

She says nothing, not wanting to admit he's right. 'What was it you used to do for a living?' she says.

'Marketing. Loathed it. I can't tell you the relief I felt on being made redundant. I always dreamed of being a poet.'

'There's always time,' she says, though she doubts there is.

'Perhaps,' he says. 'Someone once said there are only two things a poet needs, poverty and anonymity, and I have those in abundance, so perhaps you're right. Here's to the both of us getting what we want from life.' He takes another swig of rum before handing her the bottle, letting out a catarrh-shifting cough.

'The thing is, now I can't stop thinking about Pete – my first husband. All these memories flooding back. I can't stop dwelling on the past, raking it all up.'

He screws the lid on the bottle and slides it into his coat pocket. 'Ah, there's the rub: *did I live a happy life?* But that's a stupid and pointless thing to ask and can only lead to sorrow. Still, it nags away like a spoilt child, does it not?' He coughs and says, 'You don't know how embarrassed I am to be in a position that forces me to ask, Grace, but could you spare something towards a hostel?'

She opens her purse and hands him all the money it contains: £18.57. 'That's all I've got,' she says. 'Will it be enough?' She doesn't imagine for a second he's going to spend it on anything other than alcohol, but she's happy to give it.

'Blessings light upon you. That's more than generous. I am forever in your debt.'

As she lights him another cigarette, he says, 'I do hope you sort things out with your other half. It's a fuck of a life on your own.'

'That's just it,' she says, gearing up to offload. 'I feel as if I *am* on my own.'

But before she can say another word he is standing up and, with a slight bow, he whispers, 'Goodnight, sweet lady, goodnight,' and vanishes into the ellipses of the night.

DAY THREE

'GRACE?' GORDON SAYS, gently shaking her awake. 'Are you all right? You were crying and whimpering in your sleep.'

She'd been locked in a nightmare about Hannah. A young Hannah pushing her frantic way through a dense bed of roses, her face and arms scratched to ribbons on the thorns that open and close like birds' beaks, pecking at her. An earsplitting cawing that she can still hear.

'Did you have another bad dream?'

She nods and he holds her awkwardly as tears release their painful comfort. Hannah runs towards her, trips and smashes her face on the floor; teeth scattering in a spray of blood.

'I'm sorry, love,' he says, 'do you want to talk about it?'

She shakes her head and wheezes out a high-pitched, 'No,' before clearing her throat with a gruff bark. 'I'll be OK.' Hannah's bloodied face is lodged in her mind's eye, refusing to budge.

It feels strange to be this close to him; he hasn't held her in the longest time. It feels wrong, somehow. She tries to remember the last time they were physically intimate, but she can't. She allows herself to be comforted by him for as long as she can tolerate and then moves away, saddened to realise she can't trust him enough to be vulnerable with him. Can't rely on him to understand what she's going through.

After breakfast he departs, and she tries to distract her distracted mind with the local paper. But it doesn't work; she's taking none of it in until, browsing through the classifieds, she spots an advert for a medium, standing out like a clue to the puzzle her life has become. His name is Keith Kent, which doesn't strike her as much of a name for a clairvoyant. More like a game show host. She digs a biro from her handbag and circles the ad, staring at it as if waiting for it to translate into an answer. To what question, she has no idea.

She's heard her fair share of stories about ghosts and the afterlife from people claiming to have psychic powers, some gift for contacting the other side. And she's always thought them slightly deranged, people like that, or just liars, fabulists, con artists trading on other people's misery. *When you're dead, you're dead.* But, if it isn't a ghost she keeps seeing, what is it? And the more she thinks about it now, the more it seems to offer some comfort: the idea that, if it's true for Pete, then also maybe Hannah still exists in some form – on some other plane, some parallel universe, some realm of the spirits. *Maybe there's more to life than what we know, more than meets the eye*, she thinks, as she reaches for her mobile phone and dials the number.

'You're in luck, dear,' he says, 'because I've had a last-minute cancellation and could see you in an hour if you can get here.'

As she rushes to get ready she amuses herself with the absurdity of a clairvoyant not seeing a cancellation coming. Picking up the piece of paper on which she's scribbled the address, she sets off, thinking that in normal circumstances it wouldn't enter her head to do this. But these aren't normal circumstances, are they?

And so here she is, outside his house in Maida Vale, raising her hand to the glossy red front door, casting a glance to her left at the neat, colourful garden, the brightness of the flowers hurting her eyes. Scepticism almost gets the better of her, but uncertainty has left her doubting everything. It's either this, she thinks, or go to the doctor. And to go to a doctor would be to admit there *was* something wrong with her, mentally; something not right in the head. And she can't do that just yet. The smell of lithium – or rather, the memory of the smell – hits her as she presses the doorbell.

A slim, middle-aged man with extreme cheekbones opens the door. He is dressed in a lilac cheesecloth shirt and baggy white linen trousers. From a bootlace around his neck hangs a turquoise pendant.

'Grace?' he says, wide-eyed, holding out his hand. 'I'm Keith, delighted to meet you. Do come in.'

Day Three

As he turns and says, 'Follow me,' she notices his long grey hair is worn in a plait that tapers out halfway down his back. She steps inside, detecting the scent of patchouli oil and feeling suddenly unsure of what she is doing. Shutting the door behind her, she follows him along the cluttered hallway. Framed paintings and drawings cover every inch of wall space; unhung pictures and empty frames are stacked against one wall, along with piles of books.

He leads her into the front room, which is oppressively hot. 'Once the spirits arrive, the temperature will drop, so I always pop on the central heating just before a session,' he explains. The curtains are drawn, and the room is lit with a scattering of candles. She smells incense burning and nearly bursts out laughing.

'You'll have to excuse the poor lighting,' Keith says, gesturing with a flourish to the candles. 'We held a seance last night and a spirit in the guise of a monkey appeared unbidden and broke the chandelier.' He points above their heads, to an enormous glass light fixture. 'The electrician can't come till tomorrow.' He rolls hammy eyes.

Grace gives him a weak smile and takes in the room, which is as cluttered as a bric-a-brac shop. Above a marble fireplace hangs a large, gilt-framed mirror, speckled with age, just like the backs of her hands. Dark wooden furniture lines the room, bookcases overflowing with books, glass-fronted cabinets stuffed with ornaments; in one corner is a nest of tables. Every surface is cluttered with knick-knacks or more books, any spare piece of wall filled with pictures. The mantelpiece is weighed down by statues and candles and all manner of objects. She spies a small statuette of a satyr with an erection standing next to a horse's skull; Russian dolls lined up in ascending size; a small wooden mannequin with limbs akimbo. She thinks, *I wouldn't want to be the one to have to dust in here.*

In the centre of the room stands a round table, covered in a white lace cloth, and two wooden chairs. Keith holds out one of the chairs for her and she sits down, placing her handbag on the floor by her side.

He asks if she'd like a drink and when she declines he walks around to the other chair and sits down, smoothing out the surface of the cloth with delicate strokes of his hands before placing both elbows on it and lacing his long, thin fingers in front of him. She notices a turquoise ring on the pinkie of his left hand. In the bay window behind him, a large rubber plant rises from a copper pot, flanked by busts of Shakespeare and Mozart on small Doric columns.

'Now, Grace, have you ever visited a medium before?'

'No, never.'

'Not nervous, are we?'

She shakes her head and says, 'No.' She *had* been nervous, right up until the moment she clapped eyes on him; now she's beginning to regret wasting good money on this.

'Good.' He gives a big grin.

It crosses her mind to say, *Sorry, Keith, I've changed my mind*, and make a swift exit. But she doesn't want to appear rude, and besides, after seeing the ghost of her dead husband, who is she to ridicule someone for seeing monkeys in chandeliers?

'Sometimes first-timers get a bit nervous, which can give off negative energy, and that can block communication with the spirits.' Keith gestures, with a wave of the hand, to the air around him. 'And we don't want that, now, do we, dear? Besides, there's nothing at all to be scared of; I'm just going to try and pick up on any spirits that might be present around you. Before I do that, though, I find it best to get the awkward matter of coinage out of the way first.'

'Sorry?'

'The money, dear.'

From her handbag she removes her purse and hands over the two crisp twenties she'd withdrawn from the ATM earlier, watching him slide them into a trouser pocket as he says, 'Now, whilst the spirit world and the physical world co-exist, they rarely coincide. When they do, we call them ghosts. And when those we love enter the spiritual realm, they are never far from us. Yet most of the time we cannot see them, because there are enormous barriers between their realm and our own. Barriers of habit and convention; lack of sensitivity to their presence; limited powers of perception; cynicism. Whatever. Certain people, like myself, are blessed with a natural ability to penetrate those barriers and access the spirit world at will, and communicate with those who dwell there. I'm going to try to do that now, Grace, if I can. Give me your hands.'

She holds out her hands.

'I see you've been doing some gardening,' he says, looking down at the black crescents of her fingertips.

'I've got an allotment,' she says as his cold fingers close around hers. 'In Gospel Oak.' He shuts his eyes and she's unsure whether she should shut hers too, but does anyway.

He says, 'Those beings who were most important to us while they were alive on earth usually come forward first. Or those with something to ask or impart.'

The room is silent but for the hollow ticking of the grandfather clock in one corner. From outside she can hear birdsong and the thrum of distant traffic, and she is on the brink of giggles, not sure how long she can hold off.

But then he says, 'I'm getting an H,' and all desire to laugh leaves her.

She opens her eyes and looks at him; his remain shut, the candlelight throwing into relief the depth of his sockets, the gauntness of his face.

'A woman, a young woman whose name begins with H. Helen? Harriet?'

'Hannah,' she says, her voice an incredulous croak.

'Your daughter?' He opens his eyes – bright as sunlight through blue glass.

She nods. Speechless. Dizzy.

'I'm sorry, Grace. And she's very young, isn't she?'

'Sixteen. Nearly seventeen.'

'Oh, my. Too young to be robbed of life.'

She can feel a lump form in her throat. Tries to swallow, but can't.

He says, 'She's telling me you're very sad and that you shouldn't be sad. She wants you to know that she's very happy where she is.'

She tries to picture Hannah happy, but can't.

'She's with a dog. And I'm also getting an old woman. Is it Beatrice?'

'Mam's sister.'

Grace tries to think of ways he could know her, know who her parents were, who Hannah was. All she'd given him was her first name, and that only an hour ago. Despite the warmth in the room she is suddenly cold. Like some appliance unplugged, she has the feeling again of disconnection from everything; estrangement from her own being. The universe both expands and contracts simultaneously, creating a sense of insignificance that overwhelms her as she tries to imagine the moment of death: how it might feel to stop breathing, to unwind like a clock, say goodbye to life, let go; return to nothing. She pictures her corpse decomposing, until finally there is no trace of her physical presence: life measured by the slow failure or breakdown of the body, and nothing else. The thought brings both comfort and fear: the world adapting, getting on without her, as if she'd never existed at all. Does it mean anything, this being alive, this repetitive drawing of breath, this having children, this loving or not loving; this working, sleeping, putting food on the table; this suffering, the breaking of the heart? Does it signify nothing, in the end?

Remembering the reason she's come here, she says, 'Is there anyone else?'

Keith pauses, head cocked as if listening for something. 'No, dear. I'm not getting anyone else,' he says; then his cold grip tightens. 'Wait, yes, there are some others. Some old women. A few old women have appeared.'

'My aunts,' she says, dispirited, picturing them, the pixilated sisters, alarmed at how quickly she's normalised what is happening; all of a sudden this nonsense seems real. She feels exposed and vulnerable.

'Can you see a young man?'

He is silent for what seems an eternity, his eyes closed, his face as still as the bust of Shakespeare she can see over his right shoulder, staring blankly from its plinth.

'No, dear.' He shakes his head and lets go of her hands, 'Sorry. I'm definitely not getting any young man.'

'Are you sure?' She can hear the desperation in her voice.

'Positive,' he says. 'Why, dear, who else have you lost?'

So, out it all comes: about seeing the ghost, and how it has unlocked all these memories. Keith listens silently as she tells him about Pete's violence, and the circumstances of his death. As she finishes, she begins to cry. Keith stands up and walks around and gently rubs her shoulder, saying, 'That's right, you let it all out. I'll make us both a nice cup of tea,' before leaving the room.

By the time he returns, the tears have stopped and she feels calmer – and a little embarrassed.

As he places the mugs on the table, he says, 'The spirits can be very fickle, Grace. Maybe he doesn't want me to see him; or maybe the emotional bond between you both wasn't strong enough. I don't know. Are you quite sure he's dead, dear? There's not much I can do for you if he isn't actually dead, but if you'd like me to try another time, feel free to come back. Just because I didn't see him this time, it doesn't necessarily mean I won't another time.'

She takes a deep breath and reins in further tears. He says, 'My better half's a psychotherapist. I can give you his number if you'd like to go down that route.'

So I am mad, she thinks, as he hands her a business card.

'Perhaps Tarquin's your man. He's very good with grief. This ghost you keep seeing could be a manifestation of unresolved grief. You could be projecting.'

At the front door he gives her arm a gentle squeeze and says, 'If you need to talk further, just give me or Tarquin a call, OK? Don't suffer in silence.'

She thanks him and bids him goodbye, stepping out into the sunshine in a blaze of confusion. She digs around in her handbag for sunglasses and slides them on before heading towards the bus stop. Everything is suddenly too bright, too sharp, too real. She catches the bus to the allotment, Keith's words rattling around her skull like dice.

Are you quite sure he's dead, dear?

The thing is, she can't really be sure. His body was never found, after all. Perhaps he could have survived. But he'd be an old man by now, and the man she keeps seeing isn't, so she's no nearer knowing who he is or what it all means. She is more confused than ever.

It's one of those peculiar summer days when the weather can change in an instant. She had left Keith's house in blazing sunshine but by the time she arrives at the allotment black clouds have gathered in a thick herd, blocking out the sun. Sparse, heavy raindrops begin to fall, so she takes shelter in the tiny shed, curdling its impure light with blue cigarette smoke, watching through the filthy window as the grey sky empties. The cramped, dim interior comforts her, as if she's sitting inside her own skull.

THE JOURNEY she'd thought was towards Pete had proved instead to be a journey away from him, from all the grief he'd caused while alive, to the other, unknown grief of losing him. That journey she'd thought she would be so glad to see the back of, despite fearing the next beating (for she knew it would only be a matter of time, that much was bitterly predictable) would deliver things she'd never imagined. But she can't lament that past when she could see no future.

Jason was only six weeks old when they departed for Malaysia. She was already exhausted after a bad night's sleep. The baby's crying had kept her awake all night. It was as if he could sense her anxiety and was giving voice to it with his constant wailing. She knew it would be days before she could relax properly, loosen her vigilance. All morning, through dressing the kids, and getting herself ready, double-checking she had all the paperwork, she hadn't been able to shake off a terrible sense of having forgotten something crucial. Making her way through the crowds at Piccadilly Station, she could feel the irritating snag of something left behind. Going through a mental checklist, she knew it was pointless, because anything she'd forgotten, they'd just have to do without. It was too bloody late.

Hannah and Paul were buzzing with frantic energy as they boarded the train, jumping on the seats, banging on the window at passers-by till Grace snapped at them to sit down and be still. They cast a sly, fearful glance at their grandfather. Her parents were accompanying them as far as London, and she was more than grateful, knowing the children would behave in her father's presence. Hannah looked at her nervously, clutching her favourite doll, Emily, a raggedy thing with long blue and white striped legs and plaited sunflower-yellow wool for hair, which Grace had made for her, one of a batch she'd made from home to earn extra money. Hannah took the doll with her everywhere. Paul was breathing on the window and drawing faces with his finger in the condensation. Jason slumbered in the travel cot.

At Euston they were met by a sullen, acne-scarred redhead with jug ears called Ray, who said he'd be their escort all the way to Singapore. Just knowing she'd have some help immediately made Grace less anxious. After exchanging hugs and kisses, kisses and hugs, her parents went off to find their hotel. Her mother cried, and Grace cried, and the kids cried; even her father had a star in each eye. She promised to ring them as soon as she arrived.

It was getting on for six o'clock when they got to the RAF base in Hendon where they'd be spending the night in a transit hotel. Ray led them to a canteen, where they were served a bland meal of potatoes, carrots and overcooked lamb chops. Then he showed them to their room. Uniform plain corridors led on to uniform plain rooms, into one of which she followed Ray, and the children trailed behind her. He placed the suitcase down by the window and said he'd collect them in the morning. She scanned the cheerless room, spying, in one corner, a small cot into which she immediately placed Jason, who was beginning to stir, wanting to be fed.

Hannah and Paul mapped the room's insignificant territory as if their lives depended on it. One adult-sized single bed, to be jumped on and looked under; two folded-out and made-up Zedbeds to be sailed like small boats on downstream rapids; a small washbasin in one corner, with a mirror above in which to pull stupid faces while standing on the bed, by a window with dull white curtains you might like to hang on, though they probably wouldn't take your weight; and a narrow, plywood wardrobe painted regulation airforce blue. The children pulled open its door and climbed inside, rattling the half-dozen or so wire hangers and the shadows that hung from them. Grace took off her coat and pretended not to have noticed Hannah and Paul squashed inside the wardrobe; she hung her coat and closed the door. A flock of giggles arose and flew around her head; opening the door a crack again, she said, 'What are you two doing in there? Are you going to stay in there all night?' She started to shut the door on them. 'Night night,' she said.

'No! It's dark!' Paul cried, launching himself out and on to one of the Zedbeds, followed by Hannah, who did the same.

'Come on, you two, get ready for bed.'

Hannah said, 'Do we have to go?'

'Yes, love, we do have to go.'

'Why?'

'We're going to live with Daddy. Don't you want to live with Daddy?'

'No.'

She stroked the girl's hair and said, 'Of course you do, sweetheart. You're just tired.'

'Daddy's mean,' said Paul.

'Daddy loves you both very much,' Grace said. 'And, even though he hasn't met Jason yet, he loves him too.'

'Well, I hate him,' Paul said, and her heart sank as she wondered if it was too late to turn back.

'Don't say that, Paul. That's not nice.'

The night before he'd left, Pete's punch had knocked her to the floor, and she'd seen Paul and Hannah standing in the doorway in their pyjamas, ashen with fear: Paul's hand on the doorknob, Hannah clutching Emily. In a low, calm voice Grace had said, 'Get to bed – *now*!' And the two of them had turned and run, just as Pete bent down to punch the love out of her.

Now, two sets of eyes looked expectantly at her, and two sets of ears waited for her to speak.

'Get some sleep; we've got to be up early tomorrow,' she said, leaning in to kiss them both.

As she lay in bed that night, unable to sleep, she tried to find the courage to take the kids to a new life. Tried to picture herself getting the children up and dressed and slipping out of the hotel. How easy would it be to disappear completely?

Do it, she told herself. Just wake them and leave. They don't want to be with him any more than you do.

She wanted someone to tell her what to do, but knew that wasn't going to happen, which only made things worse. By morning – after a fitful sleep, the sounds of doors banging and floors creaking keeping her awake as, with pounding heart, she lay rigid and alert, imagining intruders – she knew she had no option but to get on the plane. As she stirred to the sound of Jason crying, she knew that it was too late, and her bones felt the full crush of an ossifying resignation.

After a rushed breakfast, Ray drove them to Kingston in sleeting rain. The weather reflected Grace's mood perfectly. And after boarding the plane and helping her to settle the children in, Ray went to sit at the back. For the first hour of the flight Jason wouldn't stop crying, and by the time he'd eventually cried himself to sleep her nerves were completely shredded, along with those of everyone around them. The front of her blouse was damp where she'd started to lactate. She went to the toilet to try to clean herself up, and then, while peeing, noticed specks of blood in her knickers. She cried.

Jason woke as the plane touched down to refuel in Kuwait, and when she lifted him from his travel cot he vomited the contents of his stomach over her shoulder. No sign of Ray. Feeling wretched, she crossed the tarmac, the intense humidity hanging like heavy chains around her. She bundled the children into the women's washroom to freshen up, drenched in sweat by the time she got there. She handed the baby to Hannah and searched in her bag for a change of clothing, only to discover that in the rush to make sure she would have everything she'd need for the children she'd neglected to pack any spare clothes for herself. She removed her blouse and knickers and rinsed them under the cold tap, grateful for the cool damp against her skin when she put them back on. As she was changing Jason's nappy,

Hannah said, 'Look, Mummy, a ghost,' as a woman in a black burka glided into one of the cubicles and closed the door.

She took them to the crowded waiting room, sitting Hannah and Paul down in the only two empty seats she could find. Giving Jason once more to Hannah, she poured out some orange juice from a flask and handed both cups to Paul, who managed to spill some on the jacket sleeve of the man sitting next to him. Grace apologised and tried her best to dry it off with a handkerchief from her handbag.

'Please,' he said, pushing her hand away and standing up, 'control your children,' and then, picking up his briefcase, he walked off.

She gave Paul a gentle cuff across the back of the head and said, 'Watch what you're doing!' her patience whittled to nothing. She took the seat the man had left and lit a cigarette, losing herself to the clatter and rasp of languages she didn't understand buzzing in the smoke around her. It was almost musical, she thought, this hum of voices signifying nothing to her but the sounds they made. The children sipped their drinks in silence, knowing not to try her patience.

As they were reboarding, she saw Ray ahead of them on the tarmac, and she had half a mind to give him a right bloody earful. But she thought better of it and held her tongue.

A few hours later, there was a second stop, in Colombo, and another trip to the women's room to rinse out her underwear and blouse. This time she also changed the kids' clothes. They were tired and irritable, as uncooperative as monkeys, and she cursed herself for agreeing to go, for not having the courage to leave; cursed Ray for sodding off and leaving her to cope with the kids on her own; cursed Pete for being such a bastard, and her parents for having conceived her in the first place.

Fuck life.

BY THE TIME the rain stops, Grace no longer feels like working on the allotment. A bright sun is out, making the wet leaves shimmer as she sets off back home – and just as she is passing the Prince Alfred, there he is again: Pete, sitting at a table outside the pub. And this time he isn't alone. Sitting opposite him is a young blonde woman. Grace is stripped of all certainty but this: she can't stand there staring at him without being noticed. She goes inside and orders a large glass of house white. She carries it outside, feeling like a spy and more than a little foolish; giddy, but alive with confusion.

All the chairs outside are taken, so she stands some distance away, casting what she hopes are discreet glances in his direction. She isn't near enough to hear anything they're saying, but she has a good view of his face. She's noticed that, as she's grown older, young men no longer look at her; no longer see her. At first it wounded her vanity and left her sad, but right now, she thinks, it is a blessing, for it allows her to stare at his face without fear of being noticed. His every gesture draws her back in time with increasing velocity till she is sitting with him herself, gazing into the green of his eyes, giddy on the brew of his smile, succumbing to the memory of a love she'd thought was dead and gone. She feels it creeping along the tendril of each nerve, mapping her body with its heat.

He stands and makes his way towards the door of the pub, and for a split second their eyes meet. Then the blonde girl turns and shouts, 'Luke! Get some crisps.' He nods at her and disappears inside. A seagull passes overhead, crying with laughter as Grace hurries off, no longer sure of her own name.

Gordon is watching the news when she arrives back, and she play-acts a normality she doesn't feel as she starts to make dinner.

'We've been lucky with the weather,' he says, watching her slicing a tomato. 'Are those from the allotment?'

'Yes, I picked them the other day.'

She feels the sudden urge to slice the blade into her finger just to experience something real: nip off the end, neat and swift. Putting the knife down, she breaks some eggs into a bowl.

'Oh,' Gordon says, holding up the paper, 'I saw this.' His finger rests like an indictment on the advert she'd circled that morning. 'Not thinking of seeing this crackpot, are you?'

'It's for a friend of Pam's.'

'She doesn't want to go wasting money on that claptrap,' he says, returning his attention to the television.

She looks over at this man she's spent her life with, remembering his gentleness and kindness, his devotion to her children, his sorrow when they couldn't have any of their own. Is lying to him really the answer?

She walks over and picks up the remote control; mutes the television. They look into each other's eyes, neither of them knowing what for. She sits down and says, 'It was for me, that ad. I went to see him today.'

'What on earth for?'

'Twice now I've seen Pete, but it isn't Pete, it can't be Pete. Pete's dead. Anyway, if he were alive he'd be sixty-seven, and this man is about the age Pete was when he died. So I thought it might be a… a ghost.'

The word seems clumsy and inadequate, but what other would do?

'And you know what?' she went on. 'He didn't see Pete – the medium. That's the odd thing. If I'm seeing his ghost, why can't he contact him? Or is Pete resisting? Can spirits resist?'

Gordon takes off his glasses, placing them on his lap, and strokes his face with both hands. 'Listen to yourself, Grace. You're not making any sense. There's no such thing as ghosts. How much did the charlatan fleece you?'

She remains silent. Lying to him *was* the answer.

Too late now.

'Well, however much it was,' he says, shaking his head, 'you might as well have just torn the money up and flushed it down the drain. I can hardly believe my own ears. Why would he be haunting you now? After all this time?'

'I knew you'd react like this.'

'I'm sure there's a perfectly rational explanation, Grace. But you need to see a proper doctor, not some bloody witch doctor.'

She wishes she could take the words back, even though at the same time she's glad to know now, finally, how far apart they've grown. Or perhaps have always been.

'You want your head examining, you really do,' he says.

The muted weatherman gesticulates on the television screen beside her. Suddenly frightened, she says, 'It's not like before, I promise.'

At that moment, to add to her shame, she starts to cry. Gordon stands up and for a second she thinks he is going to comfort her. Instead he walks towards the bathroom door, and she rages within, and cries even more.

He says, 'I'm sure there must be some medication they can give you for that.'

It's my heart that's sick, not my head, she wants to say.

By the time he returns she has pulled herself together enough to try again.

Day Three

'It's your understanding I need right now, Gordon, not your judgement.'

'I'm not judging you,' he says, returning to his seat.

'Yes, you are; I can see it in your face: you think I'm losing my mind again, but I'm not – honestly I'm not. It's nothing like before. It just shook me up a bit, you know, seeing someone who reminded me of Pete. That's all. It unnerved me, but I'm all right now, really I am.'

She keeps her voice moderate and light, not wanting to appear any more insane than she fears she already must, wondering what on earth had possessed her to tell him – and why the hell had she used the word 'ghost'? She looks at him and twists her mouth in a smile she doesn't feel. He doesn't return it.

'I fail to understand why you'd waste your time giving that bastard a second's thought after what he did to you,' he says.

'Forget I said anything,' she says, riven by something approaching knowledge. She clicks the sound back on the television and resumes her position at the kitchen counter.

DAY FOUR

'HOW ARE YOU feeling this morning?' Gordon says when she opens her eyes.

'I'm all right.'

'You were whimpering in your sleep again. Are you sure you shouldn't see a doctor? I'm really worried about you.'

'Please, Gordon, will you stop going on about doctors?' she says, standing up and pulling on her bathrobe. 'I think I know my own mind!'

'Are you quite sure about that? You think seeing the ghost of your dead husband is normal?'

She goes to the bathroom and bolts the door, running the shower to drown out the sobs that begin to rasp out of her. Morning light filters through the patterned glass, muting everything. There's a sudden volley of banging on the door, followed by Gordon shouting for her to come out.

'Leave me alone!' she snaps, ransacking the cabinet for some Valium she knows is in there somewhere, suddenly reminded of the day, a year ago, when she'd asked the doctor for something to help her cope. And they had, for a while. She counts them. Eighteen 10mg tablets. Enough? She takes one and replaces the box, closes the cabinet door; stares at her bloodless reflection, looks deep into the black of her pupils, trying to find someone she can recognise. She wipes her tears, blows her nose, and lets the diazepam do its subtle work as she showers. Succumbs to the dull fug of not giving a shit.

Twenty minutes later, dressed and numb, she finds Gordon seated at the table, eating toast and reading the paper. Their eyes meet, and for a split second he looks about to say something but thinks better of it. The radio plays classical music and she waits for the kettle to boil, the air charged with something she can't name. This waiting, this limbo... how many more years does she have to do it?

As she heads outside with her cup of tea, Gordon starts again. 'Grace, I really think – '

'I'm not seeing a doctor and that's the end of it. You can't make me.'

Up on deck, she listens to the radio presenter introduce the next piece of music, trying to remember what normality feels like. The sky is a uniform anaemic grey. It feels too close, too closed. Gordon appears at the door. 'Grace, what are you doing?'

'Nothing.'

'You're rocking. You're making the whole boat sway. Stop it.'

She stops, unaware she had been doing it. Tries not to look as scared as she feels. Gordon's eyes fill with unease.

'Listen, I'm going to cancel this fishing trip with Jerry.'

'What fishing trip?' she says, suddenly alert.

'I wanted to remind you yesterday, but you were so…' He leaves the statement unfinished.

'When do you leave?' she says, trying not to look or sound too elated.

'This morning. Jerry's coming here to pick me up, but I'm going to tell him I can't go.'

'When will you be back?'

'I told you, I'm not going.'

'When were you *planning* to get back?'

'Sunday.'

She counts them in her head like ripe fruit: six juicy days on her own. 'It'll do you good to have a break,' she says. 'Don't worry about me. I'm fine. Honestly, I am.'

He hadn't really wanted to cancel it at all and so he doesn't insist. 'Only if you're sure you'll be OK on your own.'

'Of course I will. Why wouldn't I be?' she says, anticipating his absence and feeling only slightly guilty for how happy it makes her feel. He too is looking more than a little relieved, she's pleased to see. He whistles as he goes back inside to start packing. And the thought occurs to her that she won't have to listen to that for almost a week.

Jerry arrives as she is drying the last of the breakfast dishes, and the two men say goodbye and leave. Once alone, she scans the empty boat, feeling like an actor blindfolded and spun on to a stage without knowing their lines. She decides to hunt down the two photographs of Pete she knows are stashed away somewhere, though she can't remember where exactly; she pulls the place apart in her search for them. On a mission. She panics at one point, thinking perhaps she had burned them along with the letters and forgotten, or binned them accidentally. They'd had to get rid of so much stuff when they'd moved on to the boat. It had felt cleansing at the time, but in the years since she's found herself regretting the loss of some things. She locates them in her Hannah shrine, inside the copy of *The Water Babies* that Pete had given to Hannah when she was born: the copy he'd had as a child.

She lays the two snapshots out on the table like a winning hand. Or a losing one. And she stares into these portals to her past with a growing sense of vertigo. Pete stares back at her in all his handsome glamour. The first was taken in Aden, on the beach. He's in a pair of trunks that leave nothing to the imagination, a Cheshire cat grin on his tanned face. When she'd shown it to the girls at work, one of them had said, 'I can see why you're marrying him!' Looking at it brings back the day when there he was at last, after those two lonely years, there in her arms with his hot nutbrown flesh and sunlight hair, making himself real again with his mouth and his hands.

The second photograph was taken on their honey-moon. It shows the two of them outside a pub on the seafront. She flips it over and reads Pete's handwriting on the back: *Isle of Wight, August '61.* They'd been to see Eden Kane singing the night before, she recalls, and were both a bit hung over. Stopping off for a lunchtime hair of the dog, they'd befriended a Cockney in RAF uniform who'd agreed to take their picture. As they posed for the camera he'd said, 'Say *dick cheese*,' which had made Pete crack up with the laughter the photograph captured.

She barely recognises the nineteen-year-old girl sitting beside him. Fresh-faced and smiling and glowing with love. *I look happy*, she thinks, trying to recall how that felt. When her love for Pete was untarnished; before the first blow; back when she would tell him she wanted to crawl inside him she couldn't get close enough, when she could still feel sheltered in his arms.

Poor cow.

The trilling of her mobile cuts into her thoughts. It's her youngest, Jason. She takes a deep breath and answers. 'Hello, love, how are you?' she says, forcing a lightness into her voice.

'Fine, how are you? I just had a call from Dad.'

'Oh, yes?'

'He said you've been acting a bit strange.'

'No more than usual,' she says, trying to chuckle but instead producing a coughing fit. When it's over she says, 'What exactly has he been saying?'

'Just that you weren't your usual self.'

'What *is* my usual self? And how would he know? He hardly sees me any more.'

'What does that mean?'

Aware of anger rising, she moderates her tone. 'Just because you spend your life with someone, it doesn't mean you know who they are.'

'You're not making any sense.'

'Yes, I am. You're not listening.'

'I'm trying to understand.'

'Well, beyond being a mother and a wife, who am I? Who am I to you?'

Taking his silence for an answer, she says, '*Exactly*. You don't know. And Gordon doesn't know, either. I'm not even sure *I* know, any more. I thought I did, but not now.'

'Why? What's happened?'

'Life happened,' she says. '*My* life. Only I feel like it happened without me, and I want it back so I can do it differently.'

'You're talking as if your life's over.'

'Maybe it is. I feel like it is. Or maybe it never even started.'

Maybe, she thinks, *maybe*, *maybe*, the word ringing in her head like a leper's bell, with the bluntness of language hitting against the fine grain of experience.

'Do you want me to come down?' he says. 'I can take a couple of days off work, or come at the weekend.'

'There's no need, love, I'm fine. You've no reason to worry. I promise.'

From outside she hears the rise and fall of a passing conversation. Then silence. *Say something*, she thinks, but nothing comes. She considers, momentarily, whether to tell him what is really going on, but before she can he says, 'Maybe you should see a doctor, Mum.'

'Don't you bloody start!' She hadn't meant to snap at him, and says in a calmer voice, 'I don't need a doctor.'

'It might help, if you're not feeling well. You know – you don't want to end up… like before,' he says.

Mad like before? Stripping off and eating soil?

'Gordon had no right to go worrying you like that,' she says, before changing the subject and asking about work. He hangs up, promising to ring again later. She thinks about his life, wondering if he is happy. Of her three children, he's always seemed the most content. He never complains about his job, or at least not to her, but she has no idea if he likes or loathes being a PE teacher. Is there a girlfriend on the go? She doesn't know. Whenever she asks he gets annoyed. She wishes he'd let her in more.

She dials Gordon's number, and when he answers she says, with barely contained rage, '*What the bloody hell have you been telling Jason?*'

'Nothing.'

'Well, you must've said something, because he's just been on the phone suggesting I need to see a doctor.'

'I thought they should know, that's all.'

'So you rang Paul as well?'

'Yes.'

'And what have you told them?'

'I'm just worried about you, Grace. No need to bite my head off.'

Day Four

'I told you, there's nothing wrong with me. I'm fine.' She thinks about that joke: F.I.N.E. – Fucked-up, Insecure, Neurotic… something.

'We care about you, that's all.'

'I'm *fine*,' she says before hanging up. Emotional, that's it. Fucked-up, Insecure, Neurotic and Emotional.

She brings to mind a woman she used to see wandering the streets back in Wythenshawe barking obscenities at passing traffic. She remembers sitting behind her once on the upper deck of a bus, watching her screaming, '*Suck shit for your fucking fare!*' and wondering what must it feel like to have so much rage inside that you lost control. *Am I losing control?* she thinks. *Shall I lose control? Would it do me some good if I did? Should I swear obscenities at full throttle? Smash something?*

A Polish friend of her mother's who'd survived a death camp – a blurred blue serial number on her wrist – used to keep in her handbag at all times a china saucer wrapped up in a tea towel, along with a small hammer. In moments of stress she would remove them, taking the hammer to the saucer until it was in pieces and all her anger had disappeared, and her face would be serene. Going over to the cupboard by the sink, Grace selects an old, chipped side plate and wraps it up in a white cotton tea towel. She takes the hammer from the toolbox beneath the sink, feeling the muscles in her right arm flex with its heft. And then for five minutes she vents her frustration by pulverising the plate, emitting deep grunts and high yelps of exertion and frustration, and cursing like a navvy under her breath. She would have gone on for longer, till the plate was powder, but when the phone starts ringing she stops to answer it.

It's Paul. She tries to calculate the time it is where he lives, but she never can work it out, even though they've been in Melbourne ten years now. 'Hello, love,' she says.

'You sound out of breath,' he says.

'I just ran for the phone; it's worn me out! Listen, Gordon had no right to go worrying you all; there's absolutely nothing wrong with me.'

'What's all this about you seeing Dad's ghost?'

'Take no notice, it was something and nothing. It's been blown out of all bloody proportion.'

'What happened?'

'*Nothing*.'

'You didn't see a ghost, then?'

'No.'

'But why would he say that?'

'So you're taking his side?'

'It's not about taking sides, Mum, it's about making sure you… you know, that you're OK.'

'I wish everyone would just stop worrying about me; I'm perfectly fine. I saw someone who reminded me of your dad, that's all. Gordon's gone and turned it into a full-scale drama. Just forget about it. How are you?'

'I'm great. Working like a madman, as usual, but essentially great. We're all doing great.' He works as a hedge fund manager, whatever that is. He's explained it to her umpteen times but all she really understands is that he makes lots of money. Lives for making lots of money. Always has. As a child he wanted to be the banker in every game of Monopoly, and would sulk if he didn't win, more than once overturning the whole board in rage.

'What time is it there?' she says.

'Ten-thirty at night.'

She asks after the wife with whom she's never really bonded, and for whom she harbours a quiet resentment for taking her son to the other side of the world.

'She's fine; we're all great.'

She asks after the grandchildren, Theda and Raffa, aged seven and five. She's not seen them since they were babies, apart from the occasional photograph.

'Did you tell them about Hannah yet?'

'Caroline doesn't think they're old enough yet.'

She feels the boat tilt with the weight of someone stepping on to it and her body tenses.

'They should know they had an auntie,' she says. 'You don't have to say any more than that. You don't have to tell them how she died.' Her voice starts to crack as her throat tightens, and Paul hears it.

'What's wrong, Mum?'

'I don't know, it's just…' She pauses at the sound of a knock at the door.

'Mum, are you all right?'

Another knock at the door, this time followed by a woman's voice calling, 'Hello?'

Grace says, 'I've got to go, love – Pam's just arrived. Give the kids a kiss from me.' She hangs up. 'Hold on a minute,' she calls to Pam, and quickly puts the honeymoon photo back in the book. The one from Aden, however, she takes to the kitchen and stashes away in her purse, though for what reason exactly she doesn't know; with every memory of her love for Pete comes a memory of how that love died.

She opens the door.

Pam is standing there with a look of concern. 'Is everything OK, love?' she says. 'What was all that smashing?'

'I had an accident.' Grace's head feels dizzy from the shame, the fear of seeming mad. 'I broke a plate. No harm done,' she says with a smile that strains to hide her nerves, wondering if she's believed. Nothing in her body feels as though it is working properly: rusted cogs and creaky joints.

'Well, if you're sure you're OK, I'll leave you to it…' Pam says. Grace invites her in for a coffee. 'Go on, then,' she says. 'Eric's out metal-detecting.'

Pam moves her large frame through the door and follows Grace into the boat; watches her lift the bundled tea towel from the table and place it in the bin below the sink. She notices the hammer but chooses not to mention it.

'So how long's he been away?' she says.

'He left this morning,' Grace replies, taking two mugs from the draining board and dropping a teaspoonful of coffee into each. In a rush of adrenalin she tells Pam all about smashing the plate. 'You should try it some time, it felt bloody marvellous!' she says, going on to explain about the Polish Jew. Becoming aware of a disturbed look on Pam's face, she looks down: she's lifted the hammer and is gently batting the handle into her open palm as she speaks. 'Anyway,' she says shoving the hammer back under the sink, 'kettle's boiled!'

She knows it's futile to try to explain what's going on inside her – she can't even explain it to herself – so she makes no more reference to it, focusing instead on giving the best impression of herself she can. And as they chat she begins to feel a bit more like her normal self again, whatever that means: enjoying this communion with another soul, even laughing once or twice. But as soon as Pam leaves it returns: that rushing tumble of liberation and panic; the creep of a leaden pain, a hurtful ache. Hemmed in by her thoughts and the walls around her, she leaves the boat and catches the bus to Hampstead Heath, needing to clear her head with its open space, to lose herself in its colours and solid air. With her heart in the grip of some eager fever, she measures out with each footfall the progress of something she is still afraid to name.

The Heath never fails to lift her spirits. Today, though, she's too weighed down with the memories and emotions that have been stirred up. Today, the Heath's green fuse pushes through her like a blade. She wanders restlessly, chewing on her anxiety, the world no longer known, no longer safe. She retreats to that first day in Malaysia.

THE FIRST THING she saw on opening her eyes was two small lizards on the ceiling directly above her, fighting noisily. At that very moment one of them shed its tail, which landed on her face, making her jump up with a scream as she swiped it away. Looking up, she saw the scream had scared them off, and remembered something from Pete's letters about how the geckos ate the mosquitoes. A mixed blessing, she thought, wondering how the children would react to them.

The unfamiliar room was filled with muted sunshine and sticky heat. Groggy from too much sleep, she looked around in search of something familiar. The skirt and blouse she'd travelled in were hanging on a clothes horse by the window and her suitcase was by the dressing table. She heard a telephone ringing through the walls, her mind a blank exhaustion of shapeless thoughts, a tangle of confused and confusing images. She could remember friends of Pete's, Norman Bailey and his blonde wife Marilyn, meeting her at the airport. She could remember getting out of the car; could picture Norman standing there holding open the door. After that, nothing but vague fragments of dreams in which Pete chased her through hot, swampy forests. She had awoken in sweats and tears, only to drop back immediately into the warm mud of exhausted sleep. There were also fragments she wasn't sure were dreams or not: someone – Marilyn? – undressing her and pulling a nightgown over her, and then a man she didn't recognise – a doctor? – sitting by the bed; Hannah and Paul standing in the doorway of the room, watching her, eyes wide with concern and confusion.

Then it came back to her, what Norman had said just before she fainted.

Easing herself into that reality, she stared at her reflection in the dressing table mirror and said, 'He's dead.' She slowly moved her head from side to side and rotated it slightly, hearing the twist and crunch of gristle. She looked at her slim arms as she held them straight up and rubbed them one after the other, observing closely, as if seeing it for the first time, the fine, firm quality and texture of her flesh.

A sudden cry from Jason stirred her, and she walked over to the cot in the corner; lifting him out, she began to rock him gently and sing him to sleep. Then, laying him back down, she went over to the window and drew up the Venetian blinds, just as Hannah and Paul burst into the room.

'Mummy!' they shrieked, rushing to clutch at her legs.

'Shush, you'll wake the baby,' she said, noticing the small, pretty Malay girl who had stepped into the room after them. She said her name was Ayu, and she told Grace that an officer had telephoned to say he'd be over shortly.

When Grace found out she'd been asleep for three days she could hardly believe it. How could she have left the children with strangers for so long? She asked if she could have some tea, then sat on the bed, calling Hannah and Paul over to join her, one on each side. 'Come on, give us a cuddle!' she said, grateful for their warm familiarity. Everything else seemed too unreal. She kissed and stroked their heads, smelt their hair, holding them for as long as they would allow, which was never long enough.

'*Selamat pagi,*' said Hannah, the first to break away and climb off the bed, running over to the window.

'What does that mean?' Grace said.

'Good morning,' Hannah said, playing with the blind, letting it drop and then pulling it up, repeatedly.

'Ayu has been teaching us,' said Paul wearily, sliding out of her arms and off the bed to join his sister by the window.

'*Terima kasih,*' Hannah said.

'That means thank you,' said Paul.

Then he started repeating it in sillier and sillier voices, shredding her nerves until she had to tell him to stop.

'Where's Daddy?' Hannah asked, but before Grace could answer Ayu reappeared to tell her the officer had arrived and that she'd shown him into the lounge. Grace asked her to take the children away and serve tea. It felt odd to be telling a complete stranger what to do – wrong, somehow – though she was grateful for the help, she had to admit. As she hurriedly dressed, she marvelled again at how long she'd been asleep.

In the lounge, a tall, middle-aged man with grey hair and moustache introduced himself as Officer George Hawkins. And as Ayu poured the tea he said, 'The day before you came, Pete was on a training mission at sea when a sudden storm broke. He was being winched down from a helicopter to pick up two men in a dinghy when lightning caused the safety mechanism to activate, cutting the winch line automatically and dropping him into the ocean. The conditions were so bad the other men had to return without him. They couldn't even see him, the waves were so high. We're hoping for the best, obviously.'

She could hear a radio somewhere playing the Mandarin version of a pop song she knew. Tried to remember the title, singing along in her head, searching for the phrase that would name it, but it wouldn't come. She was wearing the jade bracelet Pete had sent her from Aden for her eighteenth birthday. She slid it down over her hand. It felt solid and familiar, and she gripped it and looked at it.

'I'm terribly sorry, Mrs Robinson. Rest assured we're doing all we can to find him. There's a search party out there now. Do you have everything you need?'

'Yes, thank you,' she said. Her stomach was rumbling from hunger, and the mosquito bites were beginning to itch. He said, 'There's a strong chance, of course, that he's still alive. He was a very good swimmer.'

He looked awkward at the accidental past tense.

Pete *was* a good swimmer, it was true. A good dancer, too; Grace recalled, from a time that seemed impossibly long ago now, the memory of his body against hers as they danced. She thought about how much she'd loved him, and how it hadn't been enough. Because all the love in the world couldn't mend a broken bone.

She said, 'So what happens now? Do we have to go back straight away?'

He stroked his hand down over his moustache before saying, 'Not straight away. But eventually, if Pete doesn't show up.'

'Or if you find a body.'

They exchanged a long glance.

'And how long till you give up searching, or waiting?'

'This is the last day of the search, but we're hopeful he could still be making his way back here if he managed to make it to shore. You can remain here for a few weeks, but I'm afraid if he hasn't reappeared by then…' He trailed off. 'We'll need the accommodation, you see. For another family.'

It was then that the tears came, though they weren't born of sorrow so much as frustration and exhaustion, the intense physical memory of the journey she'd just completed and the sudden desperation she felt within. Then, just as quickly, the tears ran dry, and George Hawkins' relief was palpable.

He explained there was a whole new arrivals procedure he needed to go through with her, and gave her an identity card and a handbook she never did get around to reading; she couldn't see the point if they weren't staying. She knew Pete wasn't alive – could feel the world already readjusting to his absence.

'Ayu will come every day during the week, but not at weekends. She'll do housework and cook meals,' he said, handing her a piece of paper. 'This is the Baileys' telephone number. Mrs Bailey – Marilyn, will be over to see you later today.'

This, it struck her, was women's stuff: grief. Let the men play their war games; leave the women to clean up the mess. After she'd seen him out she leant her back against the cool glass of the front door, flooded with a mixture of fear and relief.

SHE'S STROLLING aimlessly across the Heath, recalling all this, when Luke steps out on to the path in front of her, nonchalant as a reed, and startling her half to death. He passes by, lost in some song playing in his headphones, sunglasses hiding his eyes.

The shadow at her feet is the only proof she's even here. The birds are gossiping and the air is still. With a strange uplift of release, like the snapping of guy ropes, something shifts inside her, and anxiety gives way to recklessness, fear to indifference. *If you see a ghost you should follow it; learn from it all you can. You may never see another.*

She stalks him down those bosky lanes, not allowing herself to think about what she's doing or why. She just walks, her head as empty as her heart is full. When the voice inside her tells her *Stop, go home, leave the poor lad alone*, she ignores it. Because she can't stop; she's too caught up in a new sense of thrill. When he turns into the entrance to the Men's Pond, though, she halts, unsure what to do. The sun is hot and there isn't a cloud in the sky; he could be twenty minutes, or he could be planning to spend hours in there. She looks at her watch: 2.35. Well, it's not as if she has anything else to do, she thinks, pushing to the back of her mind all the chores she's been neglecting. Spotting an empty bench opposite the entrance to the pond, she heads over and sits down, nearly laughing out loud at the whole ridiculous situation. Just as quickly she feels like crying.

Is this what you've become?

With the sun on her skin like a caress, she pictures Luke undressing… and then Pete shedding his clothes at the foot of the bed every night; how she'd lie there and marvel at the sight of him, recalling the intensity of the pleasure he could bring. That dark charge of desire, so long dispersed, now gathers.

The sudden sound of barking draws her attention to a young man being dragged along by half a dozen dogs of different sizes and breeds, all straining at the leash. Her gaze meets his long enough to exchange a brief smile before he is pulled away: the walker walked. A chime of blue laughter makes her look around and there is Luke, leaving the pond with a tall, brown-skinned man in a red T-shirt and blue denim shorts, a tweed flat cap on his head. She looks down at her feet: six dog-ends, crushed into pale orange commas. She busies herself rooting around in her bag, sneaking furtive glances across at them. 'It's insanely good. You have to go!' she hears Red T-shirt say, and Luke is saying, 'I will, definitely,' as they begin to stroll along the path, away from her. She stands, more alive than she's felt for a long time. It's now or never.

At the exit by the tennis courts, at the bottom of Highgate Hill, the two men turn left out of the Heath and cross the road to a parade of shops. She loiters, watching them enter a green door at the side of a newsagent's. The street takes place around her; cars pass by. Then with a jolt she sees sense, if it can be called that, and heads towards home. If it can be called that.

Making her way across the Heath, she finds herself at a fairground, its bright lights and clutter of noise drawing her into the crush, a memory of that first meeting with Pete filling her mind... the heady kisses... An impulse – a sudden, inexplicable command – directs her to the rollercoaster. She rides it three times in a row, feeling crazed but loving every minute of it, till she reaches an exhilarated rush that seems to provide some kind of release. A burst of life like a firework. The opposite of death. No longer a sad old woman, but – for too brief a spell – a teenager, falling in love for the very first time.

DAY FIVE

FOR A MOMENT Grace doesn't recognise the young woman, cannot place her at all. All she sees is Hannah's face, and a wave of disorientation hits her hard. It's the blonde from outside the pub with Luke. She is touching Grace's arm and saying, 'Are you OK?' pulling her from deep within some dark and muddy absence.

Grace looks around for co-ordinates with which to locate herself. She is in the supermarket – with no memory of even having entered the shop. It's as if she's been magically transported here. She can remember leaving the boat, but, after that, nothing. It is the oddest feeling. She becomes aware of the tight wetness of tears on her skin, wondering how long she's been standing there, by the fruit and veg, clutching an empty basket, weeping?

'Would you like to sit down?' the young woman says.

'No, thank you,' says Grace, more than a little embarrassed, 'I'm OK now. Thanks.'

'What happened to your face?' she asks, and Grace lifts a hand to touch the scab on her cheek, remembering the fall.

Day Five

She is slightly ashamed of how she'd injured her cheek. Last night, finding herself wide awake at her usual bedtime and not having any sleeping tablets, she'd swallowed six painkillers, hoping they would make her drowsy. This was on top of the bottle of wine she'd consumed and the Valium she'd forgotten she'd taken earlier. It certainly did the trick, plunging her into a full-fathomed sleep. Waking in the small hours parched and groggy, she'd climbed out of bed to fetch a glass of water from the kitchen. But when she tried to stand up she had collapsed, smashing her face on the floor and passing out. When she'd regained consciousness, unsure how long she'd been out, she'd made her way back to bed.

Surveying her reflection in the mirror this morning, she had contemplated trying to conceal the marks. She'd been good at that, once. The blood had dried, forming a scab it would be difficult to hide, so she'd decided to leave it.

'I fell. It's nothing. Really.' She smiles and the woman walks away, inserting earphones before disappearing down an aisle. Once she is out of sight, Grace puts down the basket and leaves the shop, the sense of being pursued so strong she very nearly breaks into a run. She makes straight for the Prince Alfred, wondering what on earth is happening to her. All certainties are gone, except those of the past and the losses that shaped them. The present and the future blur into a scratchy panic. The Alfred smells of polish and yesterday's beer, and at this time of day – it has only just opened – there's only a handful of customers, mainly men. She orders a glass of white wine and sits at an empty table. The only other woman in the place stares forlornly at a half-empty pint glass. The woman's age is indeterminate, her face only partly visible between lank falls of orangey bleached blonde hair with a good two inches of dark roots: the thin line of the mouth and the darkness of her shadowed eyes. Her shoulders are slumped as if all the world's sorrows weigh upon them. Grace thinks about Hannah and the pain she had been numbing. She considers approaching the woman and starting up a conversation, longing, suddenly, for some human interaction, but shyness delays her. The woman finishes her drink in one swift move and walks unsteadily out of the pub, taking her stories with her.

What happens to all the pain you refuse to feel? Grace thinks. *Does the body store it, perhaps, for a future date?*

On her way back to the boat she drops into the newsagent's for a loaf, some milk, a bottle of wine and twenty Mayfair. Unsettled by everything, and fearing she might start crying again at any moment, she needs to retreat into the boat's haunted shell as soon as possible.

She notices a luridly decorated narrowboat she hasn't seen before, and sitting on top reading a book is the blonde woman from the supermarket. Grace nearly turns back, but the girl has already spotted her and is waving hello, leaving Grace no option but to return the greeting and approach.

'You OK now?' the woman asks, closing the book and climbing down to the towpath.

'Yes, thanks. Much better.' Though she isn't.

'I'm Linden,' she says.

'I'm Grace,' says Grace, scanning the designs covering the boat's exterior: swirling spirals of vibrant colour; flowers, spaceships and anchors, stars and planets; she spots a phallus spurting like a whale. She wonders how she could have walked past it earlier without noticing it.

They both start talking at once and Linden insists Grace go first, so she says, 'How long have you been here? I don't think I've seen your boat before.'

'We've been here about a week, but we did that last night,' Linden says. 'We were off our faces and it seemed like a good idea at the time.' She lets out a short laugh.

'It's certainly distinctive!' Grace says. There is something about the brazen, primitive lines and colours that makes her want to smile. The incongruity, the difference, seems somehow to make the world a better place.

'Where are you moored?' Linden says.

'Just over there.'

'Is it permanent?'

'Yes, me and my husband Gordon have been here about five years now.' Where did the time go? What did she do with it?

'You're lucky,' Linden says, 'they're almost impossible to get.' Grace thinks of the strings Gordon pulled to secure it.

'We've got to move soon,' says Linden.

'Who else lives here?'

'Luke.'

Grace feels a sudden nausea, as if just hearing his name had conjured him, the sound of it as unsettling as his presence.

'He's out at the moment.'

She wants to ask if Luke is Linden's boyfriend, but instead asks where they are moving to.

'East, over to Springfield. Do you know it?'

'Yes, it's lovely there.'

'We leave Sunday,' Linden says, which makes Grace realise she hasn't the slightest idea what day it is, time having evolved or dissolved for her.

'What are you doing later?'

'Nothing.'

'Wanna come over for a drink?'

'I'd love to. What time?'

'Around seven? And bring your husband.'

'My husband's away,' Grace says, realising with a start how close she'd come to saying, *My husband's dead*.

Back on her own boat, she warms up a tin of tomato soup and toasts two slices of bread. Looking at the calendar to check what day it is, she notices it's less than two weeks till her birthday, *65 TODAY* written in red capitals against the date. She pours herself a glass of wine and lets her thoughts linger on the prospect of meeting Luke in a couple of hours, feeling a stupid excitement grow. The ring of her mobile dislodges her thoughts and she scrambles in her bag for it. When she sees that it's Gordon, she pauses a moment, considering whether or not to answer.

'Hello, Gordon,' she says in a gruff croak.

'You sound awful!' he says.

'Nice to hear from you too!' she says, sounding more irritated than she'd intended, her voice not yet under her command. She clears her throat.

'You want to cut down on the cigarettes,' he says.

'Is that what you rang up to tell me?'

'No, of course not.'

'How's the fishing? Caught anything yet?' She pictures her thoughts as fishes, swimming inside the bowl of her skull; pictures herself casting a line to catch them.

'Jerry has, but I've not had one bite. What have you been up to?'

'Oh, the usual.'

'Been to the allotment?'

'Yes. I'm there now,' she lies, not knowing why.

After that there is nothing to say; or rather, there is so much to say that it all remains unsaid, for fear of undoing the fine balance of their life together – even though this is happening anyway, without their knowledge, in silence and in haste. Some truth has entered undetected, like a spy under a fence, preparing to confront them both.

SHE MET GORDON the Saturday night before her departure from Singapore. Marilyn Bailey and her husband

Norman had thrown a farewell party at which Grace had had one drink too many; one minute she felt light and happy, the next nauseous. It was the first alcohol she'd had since leaving Manchester, and, already doped up on the tablets the doctor had prescribed, she had felt it go straight to her head. Stepping out on to the clubhouse veranda to get some air, she watched the fierce violence of a sudden thunderstorm cracking the night sky with flashes of blue-edged white against rolling black. The kind of storm in which a man could drown, lost at sea, weighed down by angry water.

A young man appeared, in a tuxedo and smoking a cigarette, and introduced himself as Gordon Wellbeck. 'I'm your escort for your flight back,' he said, offering his hand with a shy smile. He had crooked teeth and the kind of transparent hair that suggested he'd be bald within a couple of years. She took in his strong jaw and boxer's nose. If the light had been brighter, she might have seen the adoration in his eyes.

'I'm sorry about Pete,' he said.

'Did you know him?'

He said they didn't know each other well but had worked on helicopters together once or twice and drunk with the same crowd sometimes. From within the tales he told, she tried to extract new knowledge, a new perspective of the man she'd loved and hated with equal fire.

'I was with him in the helicopter that afternoon. A storm just like this one appeared out of nowhere. Fast and fierce.'

'Terrifying.'

'Yes. They don't last long. End as suddenly as they begin.'

'Good. I want to get back. I don't feel well.'

'I'll escort you home as soon as the rain stops,' he said, and, and, oddly, as he said the words, it stopped. Grace went inside to say goodbye to Norman and Marilyn.

Riding home in a rickshaw with Gordon, she felt safe and relaxed, though through the fuzz of drink she couldn't help thinking, *I shouldn't be doing this, I'm a grieving widow…*

The following day, unlike Ray, Gordon stuck around to help for every leg of the journey. Once the children were settled and the plane started its take-off, he offered her a cigarette and asked what she was planning to do when she got back home.

'I don't know. I'm moving back in with Mam and Dad for the time being but I don't want to be there too long. I need to get Hannah and Paul into a school. I could try and go back to work, I suppose, but who's going to look after the kids? I just don't know what I'll do, to be honest. I suppose I'll cope. That's what I do. Cope.'

She didn't want – on some level felt unable – to think about the future; it was too uncharted, too out of focus. The weeks in Malaysia had kept it in abeyance, but now it had returned, the truth slapping her in the face. The relief she'd felt after Pete's death had given way to a relentless panic about exactly what she would do now.

It was hard to put her faith in a future whose shape she couldn't properly discern. 'What about you?' she said, to divert attention from her indecision. 'Where are you off to?'

He told her he was returning to do a training course at RAF Manston in Kent. She asked him about himself, and learned that he was the youngest of three and the only boy. All his family still lived in Norwich, he said, where he'd grown up. As he spoke, she watched his full lips move and blushed to catch herself noticing.

He insisted on escorting Grace right up to her parents' house, though she'd said they'd be fine once they reached Piccadilly Station. And she was secretly pleased, grateful for his help and enjoying his company. Then arrived the awkward moment when it came to the time to part, and they both realised at once that they would probably never see each other again. A moment doesn't happen unless you allow it to, or are allowed. They both felt how unacceptable that would be, how inappropriate.

As she was considering whether to invite him in for a cup of tea, the front door opened and her parents appeared, their excited dog at their feet. And, while Grace and her mother put the children to bed, her father poured Gordon a whisky and asked about the journey.

When she received a letter from him two days later, a weird sense of *déjà vu* overcame her and she felt more excited than she had done about anything in years. The parallels with Pete's courtship weren't lost on her. In his letters were the same daily routines, almost the same cast of characters in the same billet. They weren't called 'uniforms' for nothing, she thought. But she looked forward to receiving the letters all the same, and enjoyed writing back. It felt more right than wrong to reply; felt like someone reaching out.

She didn't see Gordon again until the day of Pete's funeral service. There was no body to bury, of course, but after the inquest his parents had held a memorial service in their local church. Grace and her parents took the children, but all day she managed only five illicit minutes alone with Gordon, to talk privately. She knew her parents disapproved of the friendship, and she could only imagine what Pete's parents would say if they knew.

But the letters continued, and the occasional visit, and when, six months after returning, Grace was given a council flat not far from her parents, Gordon came up and helped with the move. That night she let him stay, though she made him sleep on the sofa.

Then, about a year after their first meeting, as they were watching TV, the kids in bed, he proposed. He told her he was thinking of taking an overseas post, but before he made a decision about it either way he needed to know if she felt anything for him, and, if so, whether she'd marry him.

He said, 'If you don't feel that way about me, Grace, I'll take the posting. And you'll never hear from me again.' And she remembered how Pete would croon, 'It's now or never,' as they'd slow-danced around her parents' living room a hopeful lifetime ago. It seemed a peculiar way to propose to someone. *Marry me or I'm off.* Made it sound like an ultimatum – which she supposed it always was.

He said he'd loved her since the first time he'd seen her. 'I only took that training course so that I could volunteer to be your escort.'

She said, 'I had no idea you felt that way. You should have said something.'

'You'd just lost Pete and it never seemed the right moment. I guess I took my time.' He let out a nervous laugh.

'You certainly did,' she said.

'If you say you'll marry me, Grace, then we can become a family. I want to be your husband if you'll have me.'

Without saying a word she went into the kitchen, recalling the excitement she'd felt when Pete had proposed – comparing it to this calm absence. There had been a time when she'd wanted this, but that time had passed. She'd often considered, on those nights he'd stayed over, whether she should invite Gordon to sleep with her. Not for sex, necessarily, though she did miss that – more a vague desire for arms around her and the nearness of a body.

As she made two cups of tea, she tried to imagine a life with Gordon, knowing that with three small children offers of marriage weren't exactly going to be a regular occurrence in her life. When she said yes, he kissed her finally with clumsy passion, as they reached for each other's bodies for the first time, with Z-*Cars* on the television and two cups of tea going cold beside them.

When she'd agreed to marry him, she'd assumed he would continue in the RAF, progressing to higher rank. Grace had liked the lifestyle, and the five weeks in Malaysia had, in particular, opened up a way of being that suited her: the climate, help with the housework and children, the ready-made social life. She had thought that in marrying Gordon she might resume that life; hoped they might even live overseas; she'd said yes to the lifestyle as much as the man. So when he announced he was leaving the RAF for a job at Ringway Airport she was furious, accusing him of having deceived her. She locked herself in the bathroom, electric with rage, unsure whether she even wanted to marry him now. She went ahead, but it was a bone of contention for years.

AS SHE TRIES to picture Gordon as a young man, the only face Grace is able to conjure is the one he wears now, and the distance between them feels monumental, all the years since her breakdown furrowed with a fertile loneliness. She feels exposed on a desolate planet. Had she cut him out or had he excluded her; or was it by mutual consent that they'd found themselves on different shores? Whatever it was, she knows their time together is over.

At around six-thirty she starts to get ready to leave After freshening up and changing into a light summer dress, she puts on an Elvis CD and parks herself in front of the mirror to put on some make-up, avoiding looking too directly into her own eyes for fear of what she might see there.

You're going to meet him, whisper the butterflies in her belly, and, excited as a schoolgirl, she grabs a bottle of wine from the fridge and makes her way over to their boat.

The sky is filled with the meaningless light of a setting sun, and Linden is sitting on deck with a glass of wine. No sign of *him*. She stands up and greets Grace with a kiss on both cheeks, which, not being a way of greeting Grace is used to, takes her slightly by surprise. She hands Linden the bottle.

'Thanks,' says Linden. 'Take a seat. I'll get you a glass.' And she ducks inside.

Sitting down, Grace spots a couple of neighbours walking by and exchanges greetings. She can almost sense their disapproval of the boat's mad exterior, probably wondering what she is doing there.

What *is* she doing here?

Linden reappears and hands her a drink. 'Luke's not back yet,' she says. 'He went for a swim hours ago. There's real time and then there's Luke time. They're very different, you quickly discover.'

'Never mind,' Grace says, masking her disappointment. 'Cheers!' They clink glasses. She takes a sip of wine.

'I'm sorry about this morning, in the supermarket.'

'You don't have to apologise.'

'I don't know what came over me. That's never happened to me before.'

'As long as you're all right.'

'I am.' She gives a fake smile.

'I thought...' Linden pauses, playing with the stem of her glass with both hands. 'Well, to be honest – when I saw the mark on your face, I thought maybe your husband had hit you.'

'Oh, God, no,' she says, not missing the irony, 'Gordon would never do that. He's never done that. No, he's away fishing with a pal. I tripped and fell over.' She thinks about how often she'd lied about the marks on her face, or the injuries on her body, after Pete's beatings. In the duration of the thought she decides against expressing it, saying, instead, 'How are you?'

Linden slumps with a weary sigh and pulls a sullen face. 'I'm a bit pissed off with myself, to be honest, Grace. I should have been in the studio all day today, but I got totally wasted last night and haven't been as productive as I should've been. I've got a show coming up and I'm really fucking behind.' She takes a sip of wine and then, more calmly, says, 'I put in a couple of good hours this afternoon, though, so I won't beat myself up too much. *Fucking superego!*' She laughs, and Grace pictures something like a comic book hero. She takes in the girl's beauty – the smoothness of the skin, the immaculate teeth and fine cheekbones – feeling a vampiric rush of desire to suck the youth right out of her. Her blonde hair is plaited now, making her look younger. Her features, Grace thinks, are almost doll-like, though there's a full sensuality in the way she is dressed: tight blue jeans and a skimpy vest-top. She thinks, *It seems so cruel that we have to grow old – like a punishment for having the audacity to stay alive.*

'What is it you do?'

'I'm an artist. A painter. At the moment I'm working on a series of anamorphic portraits,' she says, then, seeing the blank look on Grace's face, 'It's easier if I just show you.' Taking a camera from her bag, she says, 'I've got some images on here that will give you an idea of what they look like.'

She holds out a digital camera and Grace looks at the image displayed: the melting head and shoulders of a blonde-haired woman in a red dress. The face is unrecognisable, the features washed out, eyes halfway down the cheeks, mouth drooping and dripping in a sad red. In contrast, the hair, shoulders and dress – and the patterned wallpaper behind – are all finely rendered, realistic as a photograph.

'Obviously it's much larger than that. Pretty much life-size, actually. But you get the idea.'

'Yes,' Grace says, not really sure she does. Linden clicks on to another warped portrait. A figure (a man?) in a photo-real blue sequinned suit and black spiky hair, with a melted face dripping down over his collar and blue bowtie. 'Is Luke a painter too?' Grace asks, keen to learn something about him. To turn the conversation towards her quarry.

'He's a brilliant painter,' says Linden, putting the camera away. 'But he doesn't paint any more, which is a real shame. He does performance art.'

'What's that?'

'He uses his body to make art. He performs live actions.'

'Like theatre?' Grace says.

'No, not really; there isn't usually much speech or a recognisable storyline.'

'Like those living statues in Covent Garden, then?'

'Not exactly. It's hard to explain. He makes a series of images by moving the body through time. His background is fine art, not theatre. And he likes to get naked in public.'

'I see,' Grace says, thinking, *Who* are *these people?*

'In our final year at uni,' Linden is saying, 'he did this piece where he shaved his legs in a claw-footed bath in the town square in Nottingham on a Saturday afternoon. Lying there covered in bubbles wearing nothing but a shower cap, surrounded by bemused shoppers.'

'I see,' says Grace again, taking a sip of wine and trying to think of a way to respond. She isn't sure what she'd expected Luke to be; hasn't speculated for a minute on what his life might look like.

'He's performing at Given's private view this Thursday. That's the guy who owns the boat. Come along if you're free.' Grace nearly makes an excuse, never having been to a private view before, and unsure how she might cope right now in an unfamiliar social situation. But, she decides, it's about time she did something new.

'Well, I've nothing planned.'

'Great. Come here around five and we'll have a drink before heading over. Bring Gordon if he's back.'

'He won't be back till Sunday.'

She looks across the water, following the sound of a moorhen. Turning back to Linden, she says, 'Given's an unusual name,' not wanting to dwell on Gordon's return

'He's an unusual man. He's from Bristol. Black Jamaican father, white Welsh mother; both junkies. He never knew either of them. He grew up in care homes. He's six foot three and so handsome it should be outlawed.' She gives a laugh before continuing, 'His last work just won a major prize. He cast a fighter jet in butter and exhibited it in a room where the temperature was regularly alternated between hot and cold, so that the butter would melt and then reset, melt and reset till after a fortnight it was nothing but a yellow mound in the centre of the room. His work is starting to sell and he's making good money. He just bought a flat near Highgate.'

Grace wonders if it's the man she saw with Luke at the ponds, and considers mentioning it but doesn't, too ashamed of the memory of how she'd ghosted them. Linden goes inside to fetch another bottle, and Grace checks her watch, willing Luke to arrive. A flock of Canada geese honks overhead and, looking up, she sees that the mottled underside of the moon has appeared faintly in the stillblue sky like a sleepy eye.

As she refills their glasses Linden explains that Given has only recently bought the boat, but had been too busy to collect it himself. She and Luke picked it up in Hertfordshire about a month ago. She names some of the places they stopped at on the way, some of which Grace knows.

Grace says, 'How long have you and Luke been together?'

'He's not my boyfriend! He's gay.'

Grace looks at Linden's delicate, slender hand, laid out against her denim-clad thigh, and quells a sudden urge to crush her cigarette out on the smooth white back of it. Linden leans over and says, 'Can you keep a secret?'

Grace nods.

'Given's my lover.'

'Why is that a secret?'

'The first time we slept together we both thought it would be a one-off, so we decided it was best not to mention it to anyone. And then it happened again, and then again. I'm trying not to categorise what it is. But he doesn't want anyone to know. It's a fucking pain. Not even Luke knows.'

'But why?' Grace says, wanting to add, *And why are you telling me?*

'I don't know. Do you think I should be worried?' Linden asks, looking suddenly deflated. The sun has begun to drop and the sky is now a vivid crimson.

Red sky at night, shepherd's delight.

'So how did you two meet?'

'Me and Given?'

'No, you and Luke.'

'We met at uni about seven years ago. I clocked him on the first day and thought to myself, "I'm having that."' She laughs. 'Me and every other woman in the place. Plenty of the men, too, I don't doubt. I was absolutely gutted when I found out he was gay, but we became good mates once I got over the fact he wasn't going to fuck me, ever. I just wish he was more fucking punctual!'

Grace looks across the marina, longing for him to appear. Linden says, 'Are you missing your husband?'

Which one?

'No, not really. I'm quite enjoying the time on my own, to be honest.' Though she knows 'enjoy' isn't quite the right word she can't think of a better one; and she certainly doesn't want to begin describing the emotional journey of the last few days.

'Do you have children?' Linden asks, and Grace gives the barest details of Paul and Jason before mentioning Hannah, because she always does. She won't pretend she never existed, the way they do. She feels the old, familiar sadness as a lump forms in her throat. Linden places her hand on Grace's arm, looking as if she might cry herself.

'I named the boat after her,' says Grace. '*Hannah Rose*. Hannah after my grandmother, and Rose after Pete's.'

'I thought your husband's name was Gordon,' Linden says, and so, although she hadn't wanted to go into all that, Grace now finds herself having to explain.

'My first husband died just after Jason was born. None of them are Gordon's. We didn't have any together. Couldn't.' It seems like a statement not connected to her in the slightest; the details of another woman's life.

'How did he die?'

'He drowned, off the coast of Malaysia.' It feels like the kind of thing a newsreader might say. A bloodless fact.

'I'm so sorry.'

'Don't be; I'm not. By then I hated him. He was a right bastard.' She watches Linden start to roll a joint, and says, 'He used to beat the living daylights out of me. If I was ten minutes late back from the shops he'd fly into a jealous rage, asking me who'd I spoken to; had any men spoken to me? That kind of thing. Always accusing me of going with other fellas, which I never did. He thought nothing of clouting me, especially when he'd been drinking.'

'Why didn't you leave him?'

'I had nowhere to go. I had three kids! I couldn't just leave them behind, and I couldn't afford to support them on my own. Divorce was still quite scandalous back then. I didn't know anyone who was divorced.'

Linden's mobile phone lets out a trill and lights up, announcing the arrival of a text. She leans over and picks it up. 'It's from Luke,' she says, 'He's not going to make it back tonight.'

When she offers Grace the joint she declines, with a frisson of disapproval, and wonders whether to mention the cause of Hannah's death but decides against it, not wanting to dwell on it. Night has fallen and bats are now circling the trees.

Linden says, 'I knew he'd do this.'

'Oh, well,' Grace says, crestfallen, 'I'll have to meet him another time.'

She asks Linden where she is from and she replies, 'I grew up in Leeds, then studied in Nottingham for three years before moving here to do an MA at Goldsmiths, which I've just finished.'

'How old are you?'

'Nearly twenty-five.'

'By the time I was your age I'd had three children.'

'I think mine was the first generation of women to have our horizons expanded by feminism to the point where having children could become secondary to doing other stuff.'

'Feminism meant nothing to me,' Grace says. 'It was just something you read about in the papers or saw on TV. Germaine Greer, burning bras – all that. Never imagined it had anything to do with me, with my life.'

'My mum was a total inspiration to me. She's an academic and an activist. She's kinda my role model.

My younger sisters both stayed in Leeds, got married and had the two-point-four kids, which is great for them. But it isn't for me. I want something different. I've got no desire to have kids. There's no way I could handle that level of responsibility. It's unremitting!'

'It certainly is,' Grace says, starting to feel dizzy from the wine.

Linden crushes the joint in the ashtray and says, 'Actually, Grace, there was something I wanted to ask you.'

'What?' she says, finding it harder and harder to focus, concentrating on staying locked in single vision.

'Would you sit for me?'

'I am sitting,' Grace says, and Linden laughs.

'I mean would you sit for a portrait? Would you let me paint you?'

Grace pictures herself with melting features, and as if reading her mind Linden says, 'It won't be like the two I showed you. Next, I'm going to do two portraits where the faces are photo-real but the clothing and the surroundings are melting. One will be of Luke, and you'd be perfect for the other one. You've got a great face.'

Feeling a strange flush of vanity and pride, Grace finds herself saying, 'Yes. Go on, then.'

'Great. Are you free tomorrow morning?'

'I could probably spare an hour or two.'

'Fantastic. I'll pick you up around ten if that's OK.'

At that moment, Grace's vision begins to double. When she closes her eyes her head spins as if someone's turning a handle inside her skull; but with them open she can focus on nothing. All this stuff inside, clogging her mood like dirt in the mouth. Feeling a sudden surge of nausea, she leans over the side of the boat and vomits straight into the canal.

Mortified, she apologises, rummaging around in her bag for a tissue to wipe her mouth and chin, wishing she could wipe herself away like a mistake on a blackboard.

'It's OK. I'll get you a glass of water,' Linden says, putting down her drink and going inside. Dizzy and ashamed, Grace watches shadows move like serpents in the violet light around the boat, breaks in the black water giving away their location.

Linden returns and hands her a glass of water.

'I should have eaten,' Grace says. 'I think I'd better get home to bed.'

'Stay there,' says Linden, 'let me make you a sandwich and some tea. Keep drinking the water.' And she disappears back inside.

Grace feels much better after eating, but she's still too embarrassed and wretched to stay, so, insisting she is well enough to walk back on her own, she does: past the silhouetted boats like slumbering dinosaurs; or coffins laid out in a row.

Here we are, my narrowboat. For my narrow life.

She makes her way to the bed, removes her shoes and lies down fully clothed, falling into a sleep as deep as a rabbit hole.

DAY SIX

THE FAINT SOUND of knocking pulls her out into the conscious day. Feeling as if her eyes have been put in the wrong way, she climbs off the bed and flounders to the door. 'Hello?' she says without opening the door.

It's Linden. Grace suddenly remembers the arrangement they'd made the previous evening. Not wanting her to see that she slept in her clothes, she speaks through the door.

'I'm sorry, love, I'm not feeling too bright today; do you mind if we postpone the modelling?'

'Fine, no problem,' says Linden. 'Call me when you're feeling better.'

Grace makes her creaky way to the sink, wondering what happens to the dreams people don't remember. *Do they return to the deep, to resurface at another time? Or do they die, disintegrate, return to nothing?*

Ignoring the dishes piling up, she runs a glass of water, and swallows a Valium. Then she drops back into bed, pretending not to notice the mouldering teacups and encrusted plates she's let pile up around her since Gordon's departure.

If I stay in this room long enough, maybe I'll become mouldy too.

Jungled in the duvet, she maps the sequence of light changes inside the room through her eyelids, lost in a not-quite-sleeping reverie.

DURING THOSE weeks in Singapore without Pete, Grace allowed herself to feel happy for the first time in years: she had help with the children, the climate was a joy, and those little pills the doctor had prescribed made her mood lighter than she'd ever believed it would be again. She was giddy from the unexpected freedom. If she managed to avoid thinking about the future – which she did, for days on end, floating through the hours like a phantom – her current life presented no problems. Paul and Hannah spent their mornings at kindergarten and their afternoons at the outdoor swimming pool. In the evenings she took them down by the ocean in the setting sun, where they would splash in the warm surf, while she sat on the exposed roots of a palm tree with Jason. Grace strolled through those days like a sleepwalker, processing what was happening through the warm code of her children's bodies. And they so clearly loved being there.

Children had a way of grounding you, she thought. Despite – or perhaps because of – their great untamed energy, they could focus you, exhaust you, leave you no time for self-reflection. They took her mind off the blind, screaming panic over what the hell she was going to do now. While euphoria flooded her at being free of Pete, she was now a single mother wondering how she was going to manage.

Marilyn had been a godsend, helping with the children, keeping everything together, providing regular distraction in the form of day trips. Although only two years older than Grace she seemed so much more grown up and worldly-wise; the big sister she'd always wanted. She came over nearly every day, taking them out in the car (Grace couldn't even drive) to visit parks and gardens and markets. Grace recalls one afternoon in the Botanical Gardens: the yellow of Marilyn's dress, the red of her lipstick, the rich greens of the tropical foliage, the vivid flowers. The crystal sunlight illuminating everything. She remembers a troupe of long-tailed monkeys gathering around them, looking vaguely threatening as they began to chatter. Despite Marilyn's assurances that the monkeys were harmless, Paul clung to his mother's legs, whimpering, while Hannah walked boldly up to them and started throwing peanuts from the paper cone in her hand.

'May I hold him?' Marilyn had said, reaching over to take Jason from Grace's embrace. 'Norman and I can't have any,' she said, placing her lips against the downy warmth of his head.

SHE GETS OUT of bed around midday and makes her way to the bathroom; starts the shower going and watches her reflection in the mirror ghost over with condensation. She tries weighing her grief against Marilyn's: never to have a child, or to have one and bury her seventeen years later. She writes the word HELL on the clouded glass and pauses to look at it, before adding an O and then rubbing out the entire word with a squeak of her right hand.

Undressing and stepping under the water, she remembers the very first shower she ever took was in Singapore. Remembers sitting down in it for what seemed like hours, calmly crying, hardly able to believe Pete was dead.

Once dressed, she sets about cleaning the place. With Elvis playing she loads the washing machine, then fills the sink and tackles the banquet of dishes; gathers up half a dozen teacups from all over the boat, some of the older ones looking distinctly unsavoury.

Once everything is washed, dried and put away, she empties the ashtrays, wipes all the surfaces; scours the two-ring hob. Goes over the whole place with the vacuum cleaner. Finally she empties the Thetford toilet cassette. Taking the clean, damp bedding from the machine, she folds it and bags it and leaves for the launderette to dry it.

As she's passing Luke and Linden's boat she hears an almighty scream coming from inside. 'FUCKING SHIT! FUCK! CUNT! FUCKING FUCK!'

It's a man's voice. Stepping aboard, she calls out a tentative, 'Hello?'

Let it please be him.

The door opens and there he is, and time snaps like a branch against the weight of a falling body. Her falling body. Like a trick of the mind, there he is; this is him, the man who ripped her heart to shreds – more like Pete than even his own sons ever were – standing before her, wearing nothing but a pair of red shorts, holding up his left hand, which is bleeding.

'I cut myself,' he says in a gentle Scottish drawl, breaking the spell she'd been under. Putting down the laundry bags, she leads him back inside and to the sink and runs the cold tap over the cut to clean it; assesses the damage. Neither of them says a word. He smells, not unpleasantly, of sweat, and his body radiates incredible heat. It's like having *him* there in front of her. Though this one is fairer, she decides; and the eyes are a lighter green, with a gaze that seems to penetrate to the sleeping places of her soul and awaken them.

'I was opening a can of baked beans,' he says. 'They're clearly bad for you.'

It is only a small cut; the blood had made it look much worse. But it is right across the knuckle of his index finger. She says, 'Do you have any plasters?' and he shrugs.

'I don't know.'

So, while he stands there with a paper towel pressed against the wound, she rummages through her handbag and unearths a box of Elastoplast, her mind and heart racing, her sense of reality displaced entirely.

As she puts the plaster on his finger, he says, in that nutbrown voice, 'What's your name, Florence Nightingale?'

'I'm Grace.'

'You're Grace! Lovely to meet you. I'm Luke. Sorry I wasn't here last night. I was a bit worse for wear – crashed at a mate's.'

She wonders whether he knows how much the worse for wear *she'd* been last night. She hopes not. He asks if she'd like a cup of tea.

'Well, I was on my way to the launderette,' she says, hardly believing her luck, 'but go on, I'll have a quick cuppa.'

'Take a seat. Sorry about the mess.'

The boat looks the way hers had that morning. He lifts an item of clothing from the nearest seat and she sits down, taking in the walls and the wooden furniture all painted with flowers and wreaths and butterflies, figures dancing against olive green; a few posters and flyers are stuck here and there. Red gingham curtains at the windows.

He says, 'Apologies if you heard me swearing.'

'I think you were entitled to turn the air blue, given the circumstances. I know I would've done.'

Round his neck is a string of small seashells. She watches the way the muscles in his arms move as he rolls a cigarette and licks the edge of the paper with the tip of his tongue.

'Is it OK to smoke inside?' she says.

'Be my guest.'

'My husband doesn't allow it inside the boat,' she says, removing the packet from her bag. The kettle clicks off and when he turns to make the tea she notices on his back a blue-inked Icarus, tumbling in a scatter of feathers, his wings buckling beneath him.

'What a beautiful tattoo,' she says.

'Thanks. I designed it myself.'

She stares out of the window, giddy and excited, lost for words. Walking over with the tea, he points to the net curtain hanging in the window beside her, and says, 'I made that.' She'd been looking through it, not at it, so she takes in the detail of the curtain's pattern: a winged phallus, repeated over and over. 'I studied lace-making when I was in Nottingham,' he says, placing the mugs down, wincing a little from the pain of the cut. 'Do you like it?'

'It's a bit rude,' she says with a smile, and he says,

'I've given it to Given,' then, laughing at the unintentional pun, 'That's the guy who owns the boat.'

'Yes, Linden told me.'

She notes, absent-mindedly, that he has less chest hair than Pete.

'How are you feeling?' he asks. 'Lind said you were supposed to sit for her today but weren't feeling too bright.'

'I was a bit hungover. I'm not used to drinking.'

'Me too. The hangover bit, I mean, not the not used to drinking,' he says with a laugh. 'I am Scottish, after all.'

'I feel much better now,' she replies, taking a sip of tea.

'We'll have to arrange another time for you to come over before we leave on Sunday,' he says, and she is momentarily panicked. Luke and Linden are leaving. Gordon will be coming home. What will she do with the rest of her life?

'Are you coming to the private view tomorrow?' he says.

'Yes,' she says, 'I thought I might.'

This might not be happening. She's scared to let it be real.

'I'll be performing a blood work,' he says, 'so I hope you're not squeamish.'

'I've had three kids – I'm not squeamish. What's a blood work?'

'There'll be blood – my blood – in the performance. I don't want to give much more away.'

'So were you rehearsing just before I arrived?' she says with a smile, and he gives a quick laugh which makes her heart pirouette.

She notices the ladder of delicate scars on his forearms, a pale arithmetic of lines in the skin, and thinks about the kind of person that would do a thing like that.

Blood work.

Her mobile phone begins to ring and she removes it from her bag. It's Gordon. She puts it on silent before dropping it back into the bag. He looks so much like Pete and yet his voice is so unlike Pete's that her senses feel scrambled, as if everything in her life is suddenly happening all at once, past and present collapsing into a single fraction of a second, a tiny particle of time and space so explosive it could kill. She feels the sudden need to get away and put some distance between herself and this scarred young man. Standing up, all afluster, she says, 'Anyway, I'd best get to the launderette; these sheets won't dry themselves. Lovely to meet you. Thanks for the tea.'

'Thanks for the medical assistance!' he says. 'See you Thursday.'

At the launderette, she stuffs the bedding into a machine and feeds it five 20p coins. She looks at her phone. Three missed calls from Gordon. As she sits there, with her back against the warm glass, listening to the metallic rumble of the drum and the soft, rotating fall of the fabric within, she wonders if she'll have the courage to leave this one. She knows all too well that thinking about it is one thing; doing it, another.

Gordon rings again, and this time she answers it. 'Checking up on the patient?'

'I just thought I'd see how you're doing.'

'I'm fine.'

'What are you up to?'

'I'm at the launderette.'

She asks how the fishing is going but doesn't really listen to his reply. She steps outside on to the street and starts pacing up and down. Erupting within her are words she needs to say.

Interrupting him, she says, 'I can't do this any more, Gordon.'

'What do you mean? Do what?'

'I can't keep pretending I'm fine, when I'm not.'

'What's wrong?'

'I'm terrified you're going to have me locked up again.'

'I didn't have you locked up! You weren't well.'

'I was grieving for my daughter.'

'You were unwell, and you got better.'

'I didn't get better. They just stitched me back together. You don't recover from that kind of loss. You just can't. Ever. Don't you understand?' She can feel tears welling as her voice begins to crack.

'I lost her too, Grace,' he says, 'Anyway, I'm not going to lock you up. I just want you to be happy.'

'That's just it, though – I'm not happy. I can't go on like this. I'm sorry.'

'And that's why you should see a doctor. You need help.'

The need to cry wanes before any tears can come. She says, 'I don't need help. I know what's making me unhappy. Being here, with you.'

'You don't mean that.'

'I do. I'm sorry.'

'And what would make you happy?' he says, an edge to his voice.

She closes her eyes and takes a deep breath. 'That's just it – I don't know. All I know is I don't want this. Not

any more. I'm sorry, Gordon. Please don't be angry.'
I should never have married you.

He says, 'You can't leave me, just like that.'

'I've made up my mind; there's nothing to discuss,'
she says. An idea forms in her thoughts. 'I'm going to
stay with Jason for a while. I won't be here when you get
back, but I'll call you to discuss the practicalities.'

She sounds so calm it surprises her, wondering if she
seems too insensitive and deciding it doesn't matter. It
had to be done.

'Grace, please don't leave!'

'I'm sorry. I'm not trying to hurt you, and I'm not
crazy; I just need something else, something different.
Something that feels like me.'

'You're not making any sense.'

She hangs up, not quite believing she's actually said
those words. Stepping back inside the launderette, she
thinks, *So now what?* She removes the dry sheets from
the machine, folds them and bags them, suddenly fired
up with a sense of purpose. She walks to the bench in
the churchyard and calls Jason. When he doesn't pick up
she leaves a voicemail, telling him she'll be arriving in
Manchester on Friday. Here at least is a plan, somewhere
to be while she thinks about what to do next.

Back on the boat everything seems smaller and darker.
The walls lean in, the ceiling is too low; everything seems
to occupy more space than it did before. What would
Hannah have said about her walking out on Gordon?
She'd be happy for her – probably say, *About bloody*

time. But, then, what is it she wants? What will she do with what remains? Maybe a week or two at Jason's, but then where to go? All she really knows is she needs to get away – from this life; from him. Needs to find a new way of being in the world. It's become a compulsion she can't repress or ignore. And it excites her as much as it unsettles her that the details of her future have yet to be formed.

She dials Linden's number. 'Linden?'

'Hi, Grace, how are you feeling?'

'Much better, thanks. Do you want to do those pictures this afternoon?'

'Absolutely. Come by the boat and we can head to the studio together. It shouldn't take up much of your time.'

They catch a bus to Camden, where Given's studio is tucked down a side street, towards Kentish Town.

'Thank you for agreeing to do this, Grace,' Linden says, 'I've still got a way to go on the one of Luke, but it'll be good to get the photos done for yours.'

'How's his hand?'

'He'll live. He's gone to Brighton to see his family.'

'Oh, they live down there?'

'His mum does, with her second husband and two children. His parents divorced years ago, when Luke was about ten. His dad lives in the Highlands. They don't get on.'

Grace asks about the forthcoming exhibition.

'It's a group show,' Linden says. 'I'll have four pieces in it, including the one of you, so you should come to the private view. Oddly enough it's in Brighton too. Have you ever been?'

'A few times, though not for a couple of years. We've got out of the habit of doing much.'

'Then you should definitely come. It's in September.'

September seems too far away to imagine, so Grace just smiles.

They get off at Camden Lock and because the sun is out the place is packed. Once inside the studio, the first thing Grace notices is a half-built house constructed entirely from used toothbrushes.

'That's what Given's working on at the moment,' Linden says, walking over to a desk covered in books and papers. She takes a laptop from her bag and puts it down on the desk. Grace spots the two portraits she'd seen on Linden's camera, hanging next to one another on the wall, and walks over to take a closer look.

Linden shows her the portrait of Luke, which is standing on an easel. Only the face is finished: he's made up, with false eyelashes and lipstick. The rough outline of his body reveals that he has his hands on his hips, wearing a short, tight dress. Grace looks at the photograph from which she's painting, which is pinned to the easel above the canvas, and she sees that his dress is light blue. 'I'm playing around with gender in these two,' Linden says. 'He's a very pretty man and you're a very handsome woman. So I want you dressed as a man if that's all right by you.' She hands Grace a shirt and tie and a grey suit jacket.

She's never worn men's clothes before and she's self-conscious at first; it seems wrong in some way she can't define: almost shameful. Yet because of that there is also a transgressive thrill. She is testing the boundaries of a new self, and she likes it. Looking in the mirror as she knots the tie, she brings to mind her father, conjured in the tain of the glass as her own reflection takes on the contours of his face. She tries to imagine what it would feel like to go out dressed like this – to engage with the world as a man. How would it differ? Would she still be invisible? When she returns to the studio, Linden looks at her and says, '*Very* handsome!' before walking over to her bag and removing a tin of hair wax. 'Just one last finishing touch,' she says, applying some to Grace's hair with her fingertips, slicking it flat as she explains how she wants Grace to pose: shoulders back, head defiant, eyes cold and austere. 'Look as if you own the world,' she says. 'Lord of fucking everything.'

She gives Grace various objects to hold: a tall, slim lime-green vase, a leatherbound book, a pipe, the smell of it conjuring her father again, or rather the absence of him – her paltry knowledge of him. After her initial awkwardness, Grace relaxes into the posing, enjoying this make-believe, this mask of masculinity. *Is this how it's done?* she wonders. *Do they act at being men, learning from other men, from their fathers?* And was that what she'd done: play-acted at being a woman, performing a femininity learnt from her mother and other women?

Linden hands her a cut-throat razor and says, 'Finally, can you hold this like you're either about to shave or slit your own throat?'

Afterwards, on the bus, Linden points to the ring on the third finger of Grace's right hand: a small silver snake, its tail disappearing into its mouth.

'I like your ouroboros ring,' she says.

'What did you call it?'

'Ouroboros. The snake that eats its own tail.'

'I never knew it had a name,' Grace says, pleased to learn this new fact. 'It was Hannah's. I've worn it ever since she died.'

SHE WAS IN the house on her own when the police called, preparing the evening meal before the arrival of Gordon and the boys. She'd long since stopped setting a place for Hannah, though the exclusion still pained her; but this evening she'd found herself automatically setting an extra place, and it was in that split second of awareness of what she'd done that the doorbell rang.

As soon as she saw the uniforms she knew Hannah had used up her nine lives.

She let out a loud wail when they told her. While the WPC made a cup of tea, Grace rocked and keened, oblivious to the presence of others. A world of untold pain had claimed her. When she asked them how she had died, the male PC said, 'Dodgy heroin,' as if it happened all the time, which it probably did.

But not to me. Not to me.

She wanted to slap him.

'HOW DID she die?' Linden says.

Grace hadn't wanted to talk about these things. Finds it hard to talk about these things. The nausea of the moment returns, for the body remembers things, too.

'An overdose.'

'Oh, Grace, how awful!'

'She was a drug addict. Left home at sixteen and we had no idea where she was.' She feels as if she wants to talk and never stop, tell Linden everything. Lay it all out like the bones of a dinosaur; watch them gradually assume their extinct shape.

Linden says, 'When I was seventeen my boyfriend was hit by a train while walking home along the tracks one night. I always told him not to go that way and if we were together I made us go the long way. But he was on his own that night and pissed.'

Grace says, 'I'm sorry,' thinking how odd it was that custom makes us apologise for things that aren't our fault.

'I've no way of knowing if it was suicide or just a stupid accident. Because he used to get very low, used to talk about ending his life, but I didn't believe he'd ever do it.'

Grace says, 'I remember taking the kids to Chester Zoo once when Hannah was about six. And she was in such a glum mood as I was getting them ready, I tried to cheer her up telling her about all the animals she would be seeing. And when I mentioned bears she said, "Good, I can chuck myself in the bear pit."'

'Christ!'

'I didn't let her out of my sight all day. She used to have these really sullen, withdrawn moods. "Putting her funny hat on", we called it – trying to make light of it, I suppose – but she did worry me sick, always looking so tortured.'

Each word uttered seems like an insignificant fraction of what she wants to say, and yet at the same time it feels like a victory. A knowledge imparted; a poison drained.

When they get off the bus, Grace announces she isn't going directly home and they part company. Earlier, at the studio, watching Linden use a laptop to go online and find an image she wanted to reference, an idea had formed in Grace's head, so she makes her way to the local library to do some research of her own.

Grace is familiar with the library but she has never used the internet before, so she goes over to the help desk – which is manned, she sees from the name badge on his lapel, by Lazlo, a gaunt, bouffant-haired man of about sixty decked out in a colourful cravat and navy blue pocket-crested blazer. His fishblue eyes are reduced to bright beads by thick tortoiseshell glasses fringed across the top with unkempt eyebrows. In his slow, mannered Slavic accent, Lazlo talks her through the whole procedure, and once he's gone she types in the words 'luke performance artist london', which yields several images of him naked and/or covered in blood, plus the surname – Murphy – but nothing more.

Then she types in 'artist given london' and in no time at all there he is: the man she'd seen with Luke at the ponds. She's sure of it. She takes in what had evaded her then: the fine brown features and beautiful eyes. Lashes like a girl's.

She finds details of his exhibition, *All There Is Plus All There Is Not*, at the Looking Glass Gallery on Redchurch Street, Shoreditch. There are photographs of his work but she doesn't pay much attention. She reads an interview with him from the *Guardian*, in which he speaks about his difficult childhood being moved around between care homes, and about his encounters with racism and how he believes that not knowing his parents has informed everything he does, 'as though my life and my art are both some kind of search for origins, for a starting point, for a place to begin'.

On a whim she does a search on the name 'pete robinson', but that only generates a rogue's gallery of strangers it would take hours to trawl through, and besides, what the hell does she think she is going to find? But then she adds the words 'RAF 1950s 1960s' to the search, and before long she's unearthed an image of him, from his days as a Boy Entrant in 1956, two years before she met him. It's a grainy black and white group shot taken outside a billet in Bassingbourn. He's sitting on the grass, front far left, cigarette in hand; relaxed and indifferent, unlike the more formal poses of the men with him. Some of them are named, but not him, though she knows in her blood and her bones – even though he is staring down at the ground and not at the camera – that it's him. It unnerves her almost as much as if he'd been standing right behind her.

She types in 'Singapore 1967' and spends a good two hours or so revisiting the past in photographs and stories from other people's time there in the Forces. She can almost smell the monsoon drains; feel the cool of the tiles underfoot; see Ayu's kind face. Memories she had folded up and hidden away come back to her vividly, till she's back in that heat with its rattling ceiling fans and chit-chattering geckos.

FREED FROM Pete's tyranny, she felt a kind of freedom she hadn't dared to hope for. Like a dream come true, in many ways, it seemed to her at the time. And the children thrived in the warmth and the sunshine, getting used to the chit-chats, even giving them names and treating them like pets.

She explained to the children as best she could what had happened to their father, that he wasn't coming back, but she had no way of knowing how much they understood. *At what age does death start making sense?* she wondered. *Do we move from ignorance to knowledge in one tragic instant when the full impact hits?*

She allowed life to slide into a calm routine, never thinking about Pete at all, though almost every night would find her locked inside vivid and intense sexual dreams of him which left her missing his body on her body, in her body, a loss only accentuated by the incessant heat surrounding her.

WHEN THE LIBRARY closes, she makes her way home, feeling as though she's returning from a long trip away. Back on the boat she sits down in front of her make-up mirror, wishing she could claw her skin off; dig deep into her flesh and excavate the young woman buried there.

The evening gapes empty ahead of her, a nest of hours like open mouths waiting to be fed. Halfway through her second glass of wine she starts searching the phone book for the number of a local hair salon. She calls and makes an appointment for the following morning. Just in time for the private view.

'So, you're going, then?' she says to the mirror.

Or did the mirror say it to her?

DAY SEVEN

THE NEXT MORNING Grace wakes early, feeling more refreshed than she has for a long time. On the bus on the way to the salon she wonders what hairstyle to ask for. She hasn't been to the hairdresser's in years; since moving on to the boat she's cut it herself to save money, keeping it short and manageable. Her only certainty is a pressing need for change. Linden's comment about her looking androgynous has made her self-conscious; her attraction to Luke has made her vain. The combination of the two has brought her here.

After seating her with a coffee, Dylan, her stylist, suggests strawberry blonde might suit her.

'I don't want to look like mutton dressed as lamb,' she says.

'Don't worry, it's a very soft blonde. Very flattering. Here, have a look.' And he hands her a magazine. 'See? I think it'll really suit you.'

'OK, but not too much taken off. I'm growing it.'

'No worries,' Dylan says, 'I'll just chop it up a bit.'

As a junior washes her hair, she finds herself enjoying the pampering and the welcome distraction from her anxieties about the private view. When she's back in the chair, Dylan sets to work. Above the crisp snip of the blades he says, 'Is it for a special occasion?' She tells him all about the private view, and about modelling for Linden, and then, worried she is doing what her mother would call 'showing off', she clams up, feeling at the mercy of her oscillating moods more than ever before.

She treats herself to a facial – *no pockets in a shroud* – and two hours later she walks out feeling, and looking, years younger. She can't seem to stop seeking out her reflection in shop windows, beguiled by the wild-eyed woman staring back from the glass. Can she trust her? If she follows this person, where will she take her?

In the window of a Cancer Research shop a dress catches her eye. Its pattern – a storm of purple, orange, white and blue swirls – reminds her of one she once made centuries ago. She goes inside and tries it on. It fits her perfectly, as do the pair of shoes – blue, with a moderate heel, hardly worn – that she also buys.

She is back on the boat just after 1.30pm. She packs a small case to take to Jason's tomorrow morning. The remainder of the restless afternoon is spent pacing the corridors of that dead time before having something to do. She tries reading a book, but the words play truant. She gives in and pours a glass of wine to take the edge off her nerves. No word from Gordon, thankfully.

As she showers and changes into the new dress, her mood becomes more buoyant. She pulls on a black jersey cardigan and selects a maroon pashmina scarf purchased at Camden Market on Jason's last visit. As she puts on some make-up she feels a giddy twist in her stomach thinking about Luke.

Daft cow, the mirror says, and the wine glass agrees.

Just before five o'clock, she heads over to their boat, and it gives her heart a lift to see him as she approaches. He looks up from his book and says, 'My God, Grace, you look amazing. I love your hair,' standing up and making her heart light up with a kiss on both cheeks.

'Wow,' says Linden, appearing from inside, 'it's taken years off you.'

'A change is as good as a rest,' Grace says.

Linden pours her a drink as Luke tells them about the trip he just made to Brighton for his sister's sixteenth birthday party. *Hannah's age when I last saw her alive*, Grace thinks with the flinch of a quick, sharp sorrow.

She asks Linden how the painting is coming along.

'The photos we did all look great, and I think I know which one I'm going to use, but I just haven't had any time to finish the one of Luke. I've been too busy helping Given hang his show.'

'So, he's well hung!' Luke says with a laugh.

'I decided to use the one with the pipe. It looks very Radclyffe Hall.'

Who? Grace thinks, but says nothing.

Just after six they take a taxi to Shoreditch, a part of London Grace has never been before. As Linden and Luke discuss people she doesn't know, she sinks back in the seat and tries to relax, looks out at the unfurling streets, full of life, excited to be out tapping the city's energy. There'd been a spate of going to places during their first two years in London – shows in the West End, galleries and museums, the odd concert. She had loved it, but it was expensive and they'd had to cut back. She realises now how much she misses it.

A text message from Gordon arrives: *I'm coming home*. The thought of him returning makes her panic. She replies: *Please don't*, before switching her phone off and resolving to get an early train tomorrow. The last thing she wants is him getting back before she's left.

Outside the gallery people are gathered on the pavement, talking and drinking. A motley crew, she thinks, though she's relieved to see a few older faces; one of her biggest worries had been that she'd be the oldest person there by a couple of decades. As Luke pays the cab driver, Linden goes inside to get drinks. Grace lights a cigarette and pushes Gordon to the back of her mind.

She asks Luke about the cut on his hand.

'On the mend. I'll take the plaster off for the performance. If it starts to bleed, all the better.'

He seems distracted, scanning the crowd.

'What time are you performing?'

'Eight.'

She notices his eyes change, as if a light has just come on behind them, and when she turns and follows his gaze the penny drops: it's Given. He's in love with Given. Of course he is. Just then, Linden appears with three glasses of wine, and the world imperceptibly turns.

Day Seven

Given comes over and kisses them, thanking them for coming. As he starts to roll a cigarette and chat about who's there, Grace studies him. He looks no better than he should, as her maternal grandmother would have said. Good-looking and knows it. She steps inside the gallery to see what all the fuss is about.

Each wall in the room is decorated entirely, floor to ceiling, with different strips of wallpaper: no two patterns are the same. Each strip is emblazoned with a phrase or sentence, each in a different typeface, some florid, others simple. One or two are in black marker pen. Grace walks around the space slowly, reading each one.

WE KNOW OF THE WORLD WHAT WE SEEK OF THE WORLD.

THE LOST OBJECT IS THE ONE THAT NEVER REALLY GOES AWAY.

ALL THIS I AM AND WANT TO BE: AT THE SAME TIME DOVE, SERPENT & PIG.

CONCEIVING UTOPIAS IS ONE OF THE FEW ADVANTAGES OF BEING ABLE TO THINK.

Like voices from inside her own head, these words unpack their wares. Some she reads more than once, trying to extract meaning, or just explore how they make her think and feel.

GLORY IN THE FICTIONS OF SELECTIVE MEMORY –
WE FORGET BECAUSE WE MUST AND NOT BECAUSE
WE WILL.

TECHNOLOGY IS THE FUEL CAPITALISM BURNS.
HUMANITY IS THE FUEL TECHNOLOGY BURNS.

She has no idea if the words are original or appropriated. Some mean nothing to her at all, and some move her profoundly.

IS IT MADNESS OR REASON THAT BEST EXPRESSES
THE TRUTH?

THE TRUTHS OF MY GRIEF ARE AS PURE AND
INDISPUTABLE AS THE AXIOMS OF MATHEMATICS.

WE ARE ALL RECIDIVISTS; IT IS SIMPLY A QUESTION
OF DISCOVERING OUR CRIME.

Linden appears beside her, holding out a bottle of wine.

'So what do you think?' she says, refilling both their glasses.

'It's just wallpaper.'

Linden laughs and says, 'I meant about Given.'

Grace thinks he seems a bit full of himself, but she doesn't like to say. *Handsome is as handsome does.*

'He seems nice enough,' she says.

'I think Luke's got a bit of a crush on him. Have you noticed the way he looks at him?'

'No, I can't say I have,' she says, looking away, over Linden's shoulder, to where she can see the two young men outside, standing close and deep in conversation. Given's back is to her, but she can see Luke's face, aglow with attentive love. She hopes her own infatuation isn't so apparent.

'I fucking hate all this secrecy,' Linden says.

'What a tangled web we weave,' Grace says, spotting Given break away from Luke and enter the gallery, making his way towards them. Her gaze lingers on Luke's crestfallen face. 'Speak of the devil,' she says, and takes a sip of wine.

'So, Grace,' Given says, 'what do you think of the work?'

'She thinks it's just wallpaper,' Linden says.

'Well, it is, isn't it?' Grace says.

'It is, Grace,' he says with a smile. 'But imagine if walls could talk. What might they say about what they've observed?' Turning to Linden, he asks if he can have a word in private.

'*Don't fish for compliments in polluted waters,*' she says, as he leads Linden away, and through a door in the back wall. 'I like that one.'

Just before eight o'clock, people begin to move inside for Luke's performance, gathering around a white enamel bath in the centre of the room, half-filled with water.

From a winch in the ceiling hang two metal chains, ending about a foot above the water. A slow, deep pulse of electronic noise starts, and Luke appears from a door at the back of the gallery, wearing nothing but a black leather harness. Down each arm and each leg run a row of horizontal white feathers piercing the skin, with two on either side of his forehead. With measured steps he walks towards the bath, and as he gets closer Grace can make out the full scarlet red of his painted mouth. His eyes are intense, his face more serious than she has ever seen it. She avoids looking directly at his genitals for as long as curiosity and desire allow.

Stepping into the bath, he grabs the two chains and attaches them to the harness. The chains begin to winch him up slowly until he is suspended above the bath, his toes just clearing the surface of the water. He starts removing one of the feathers from his forehead, dropping it into the bathwater below. One by one he removes each feathered needle, and blood begins to run down his face, his chest, his arms, his legs, dripping into the bathwater, where it blossoms into scarlet plumes; and all the while the room is filled with a slow metallic music, like a sleeper's heartbeat. As the feathers collect on the water's crimson meniscus, all Grace can see is a five-year-old Hannah sitting there, razor in hand, with Jason by her side, covered in blood.

The sound of applause snaps Grace back to the present. Luke is now back on the ground, walking slowly towards the door from which he'd appeared, Icarus partially visible between the straps of the harness. Time has passed, of which she has no memory; a cigarette burn in the fabric of her consciousness.

And her eyes are wet with tears.

Please, not here.

What is she doing here? What is she hoping to find?

Making her way outside, she reads a strip of wallpaper by the door: MY BODY IS A CEMETERY PACKED WITH WEEPING GHOSTS.

She lights a cigarette, unable to rid herself of the image of Hannah with a razor in her hand; her defiant face. She considers whether she shouldn't just go home; but the thought of being alone terrifies her. As she's grinding out her cigarette butt, she sees Luke walking towards her, changed back into his clothes. She asks him where the toilet is and he says, 'Come with me,' leading her back into the gallery into a small office with a desk and a computer, shelves filled with books and ring binders. He points to a white door. 'Through there,' he says.

She returns to find him pulling open the desk drawers in search of something. He says, 'I know there's some booze in here somewhere – ah!' And he holds up a half-empty bottle of Jim Beam and plants a kiss on it.

He picks up the leather harness from the sofa and places it on the desk, so she can sit down. He sits next to her, and she stares at the marks on his forehead where the feathers punctured the skin, wondering if it had hurt. He pours them both some bourbon and asks what she thought of the performance. She still finds it hard to look at him, impossible to hold his gaze – though in truth that's all she wants to do. She looks down at the carpet as she tells him what Hannah did to Jason.

'I've no idea why she did it. I only left them for a minute to answer the phone. Luckily they were only minor cuts. He didn't need stitches and there were no lasting scars. Thank God. So, I found the performance a bit harrowing.'

'Does Jason remember it?'

'I've no idea.'

'How old was he?'

'Just over a year, so young enough not to remember, I hope.'

'My earliest memory is from around three years old. I can remember moving into a new house.'

'I can remember being in a pram, which is very young, but only vaguely. I hope he doesn't remember, but I'm scared to ask him. If he's forgotten, I'd rather he didn't know she did that.'

Luke says, 'And what do you think of Given?'

'All right if you like that kind of thing,' she says.

'I *do* like that kind of thing!' He moves in closer. 'Oh, fuck, Grace, I'm so in love!' he says, letting out a hopeless laugh and beaming with joy. 'Don't you think he's the most beautiful man you've ever laid eyes on?'

She feels a pang for something lost: the man she thought was a dream come true, once upon a time; her prince, her knight in shining bloody armour.

'And he's hung like a fucking canal barge,' he says, and she looks at his mouth as he speaks, at those lips she used to love kissing.

'But you mustn't tell anyone,' he says.

She suddenly feels protective towards him, wondering whether or not to tell him. A fleeting cruelty makes her want him to suffer, to see his heartbreak, his tears; reveal to him the truth about his wonderful God's gift.

'Why don't you want anyone to know?' she says.

'It's not me, it's him,' he says. '*I* wanna tell the whole fucking world, shout it from the fucking rooftops, but Mr Closet Case out there is worried about people knowing. God knows why! It's not as if anyone would give a shit.' He takes an angry glug of bourbon and looks at her. 'Anyway, I've decided: tonight I'm gonna force his hand. If he won't tell *Linden*, at least, I will.'

The door opens and as if on cue Linden's head appears. 'There you are,' she says to Luke. 'There's someone here who wants to talk to you.'

'I'll be right back, Grace,' he says, standing up and heading for the door. 'Don't move.'

She resolves to leave as soon as she can. The memory of Hannah's sly cruelty has unnerved her. She thinks about that time, around the age of eleven, when she'd caught her tormenting their cat. She'd cornered it at the foot of the stairs, where it hissed and wailed with fierce terror. When Grace had asked why she'd done it she'd replied, with a shrug, 'I don't know.' And, although she'd said no when Grace asked if she'd done it before, there was no way of knowing for sure.

Them she started faking suicides. Grace would find her collapsed on the floor with a pill bottle in her hand, none of which she ever actually swallowed. She only stopped doing it when Grace threatened to take her to a child psychologist. Then she took to running away instead. The whole family would be out looking for her. More than once the police brought her back, one time after finding her on the hard shoulder of the motorway, thumbing a ride. There seemed no way of controlling her. She did just as she pleased.

The minutes pass, and, fed up with waiting for Luke to return, Grace leaves the office, spotting him straight away, on the other side of the room, talking to a smaller young man in tight black jeans. She makes her way over, and by the time she gets there Luke is bidding the man goodbye. 'I was just about to come back and get you,' Luke says to her.

'How did it go?'

'He wants me to go over to Berlin and perform at this live art festival in a couple of months. All expenses paid, plus a good fee. It's a really brilliant festival. I've been before, but never to perform. I'm psyched about that.'

'Will you do the same thing?'

'I doubt it. I never do the same piece twice.'

A small tattooed girl with a large black beehive appears and announces, as if someone has died, that there is no more wine. Luke introduces Grace, and the girl kisses her on both cheeks and says, 'Nice to meet you. I'm Frankie.'

'I love your tattoos,' says Grace.

'Thanks, they love you too,' she says.

Her strapless dress reveals across her chest a skull and crossbones wreathed in red roses, a scroll beneath it bearing the words *Sapere Aude*. Grace asks what it means.

'Dare to know,' Frankie says.

'Dangerous to know, more like,' Luke says, placing his arm across the girl's shoulders.

'Too right,' Frankie says, sinking her teeth into Luke's upper arm and snarling like a dog.

'Let's go to the Golden Heart,' says Luke, downing the dregs of a bottle of beer. 'Wait here while I collect my bag and tell the others.'

As he walks away Frankie says, 'Why are all the hot men gay? Such a waste! Mind you, from what I hear *none of that* goes to waste!' She cackles and Grace smiles, remarking that she likes Frankie's dress.

'I used to have one a bit like it. I made all my own dresses when I was your age,' she says. 'And my hair was just the same as yours, back then. It's a bugger to do, isn't it?'

She remembers how Paul and Hannah used to sit and watch her backcombing her hair; how she'd turn to them when it was spiking out from her head and pull a witchy face and they would squeal and run away as she chased them. The memory makes her smile.

Frankie's attention visibly shifts to a tall man in a baseball cap who is just that second walking by. 'See you at the pub, Grace, yeah? Lovely to meet you!' she says, blowing a kiss as she runs to catch up with the boy.

Luke reappears with Linden, who says, 'Given's going to join us there.'

'I think I should be getting back,' Grace says, afraid of what might happen if she stays. She doesn't want to be there when the shit hits the fan. 'I'm tired.'

'Nonsense,' says Luke, holding out his arm. 'Come for one.'

And before she can resist they're off, the three of them, Linden taking her other arm.

The Golden Heart is crowded, inside and out. It's a balmy night, and the sky is only just beginning to darken, revealing stars that seem brighter than usual. Luke and Grace stay outside while Linden goes inside to get drinks. A loud peal of laughter causes a sudden sting of paranoia: perhaps everyone can tell how lovelorn she is. She tries to shake the thought away, but like a persistent wasp it keeps returning.

An hour later she and Luke are walking down the dimly lit backstreets of Hackney Wick on their way to a squat party, with Linden and Given and a band of others closely behind. She feels as though she's run off to join the circus; the quick, sharp humour bubbling around lifts her spirits. She hasn't laughed like this for aeons. She feels drunk and in love, and, even though a tiny voice keeps berating her and commanding her to go home, she ignores it, following Luke like an enraptured child dancing to a piper's tune.

The party is in an old red-brick garage with a two-storey flat above. They enter through a large covered forecourt filled with old sofas and rugs. Men and women, some, to Grace, looking like no more than children, sit around drinking and chatting. A grey-haired man in a tartan suit approaches Luke and embraces him with a kiss. Next to him is a shorter man with bleached hair, in jeans and a T-shirt. Luke introduces them to Grace as 'the two Richards'.

'Or the two Dicks,' the blond one says with a laugh. 'I'm Dick One and she's Dick Two.'

Giving Grace a wild-eyed Joker grin, Dick Two says, 'Is this the woman we need to thank for your very existence?'

Luke says, 'No, this is Grace; she's a friend.'

'*Enchanté*,' he says, taking her hand and kissing the back of it.

'Likewise,' says Dick One, repeating the gesture.

Dick Two removes something from his jacket pocket, holding out to Luke two small clear plastic bags of white powder. 'One of these is ketamine and the other's cocaine but I'm too fucked to tell the difference,' he says.

Grace's mood shifts to panic at the mention of drugs. The berating voice inside tells her smugly that she should never have come. She turns a deaf ear to it, determined to stay in a buoyant mood. Showing no sign of her internal conflict, she watches Luke take one of the bags and tease it open with expert ease. He licks the tip of his little finger and jabs it inside; sticks his finger into his mouth. 'That's the K,' he says, closing the bag and handing it back. Holding up the other, he says, 'May I?'

'Be my guest,' says Dick Two. 'And count us in.'

While Dick One goes off to get drinks they sit down at an empty table. Grace looks around for Linden and Given and the others they arrived with, but they're nowhere to be seen. As Luke starts to cut lines of cocaine, Grace once again feels the rub of discomfort, but then Dick One returns with four glasses of punch, and the four of them clink cheers, and she smiles and takes a swig to ease her mood. 'Don't use the bogs,' Dick One says, 'they're rank. I went to reapply my lippy earlier and I dropped it, and what I picked up thinking it was my lipstick was in fact a dried-up old cat turd. Luckily I noticed before it actually touched my lips.'

'Pay no attention to her,' says the other, 'she's taken far too much ketamine. Any minute now she'll be in Ancient Egypt, thinking she's Cleopatra.'

Dick One stares at Grace wide-eyed and says, 'I love your pashmina!'

She looks at his tight yellow T-shirt and reads the slogan across his chest: *Not Gay As In Happy But Queer As In Fuck Off*. She gives him a smile and says, 'Thank you.'

'How many lines am I cutting?' Luke asks, and they all look at Grace.

'Go on,' Dick One says, 'it's quality stuff.'

'No, thanks,' she says, imagining a police raid.

'Eminently sensible,' says Dick Two, returning the bag to his pocket.

She watches the three men lean and sniff in turn, and wonders what kind of world she's tumbled into. 'Have any of you ever taken heroin?'

'What do you think I am, a *drug addict*?' Dick Two says in mock horror, clutching at invisible pearls. 'I didn't have you down as a junkie, Grace, but I can get you some, no problem.'

'I don't want any! I was just curious,' says Grace, horrified.

'Ah, the oysters were curious too,' he says, running his hand through Luke's hair and twisting it around a finger. 'Anyway, Heartface, you were amazing tonight, just amazing,' he says. 'I wanted to rush over and lick your wounds – provide succour, if you'd let me.' He strokes Luke's face.

'Behave,' Luke says, pushing the man's hand away.

'So when are you next getting naked in public? I mean, performing,' Dick Two says with a helium grin.

Across the room Grace sees Frankie chatting to Baseball Cap and for some reason it makes her smile. She feels attuned to all this bright energy around her. It is the fullest, truest smile she's offered for a long time. 'What is this drink?' she says, emptying her glass. 'It doesn't half taste weird.'

'It's Mandy Punch,' says Dick One. 'Has it kicked in yet?'

'What's that?'

'Vodka with mandy in it, innit, babes.' Seeing the blank look on her face, he adds, 'MDMA. Ecstasy.'

'Fabulous,' says Dick Two, clapping his hands in glee.

'*I don't take drugs. I'm sixty-four!*' she says.

'Nonsense,' he says, 'I've always said Ecstasy should be available free to the elderly. Old age is no place for sissies. That's when you need them most. Just relax and enjoy the high.'

She stands up, clutching at her handbag as if one of them might try to steal it. 'Can you call me a taxi, please, Luke?' she says. 'I want to go home now.' She walks away and makes her way out on to the street, panicked and furious. There is no traffic, and the night is still, the only sound the muted beats from the party and the rumble of speech that comes from too many people all talking at the same time.

Luke appears. He says, 'Grace, are you OK?'

'What the bloody hell are you doing, giving me drugs?'

'I didn't know there'd be mandy in it! You're OK, aren't you?'

'I don't want to take drugs!' *Drugs killed my Hannah.*

'Listen! Relax!' He approaches her and wraps an arm around her shoulder. 'You didn't have much of it; you'll be fine, I promise.'

'What will it do to me?'

'Well, how do you feel?'

She takes a deep breath. It's nice to feel his arm around her. Despite herself a smile pushes its crafty way on to her face. *So this is it*, she thinks. *This is what the drugs do*. For the first time since arriving at the private view she doesn't feel out of place, or misplaced. She feels aroused and more alive than she's felt in years, perhaps in her entire life, all her previous anxieties now gone, replaced by an alert and invincible joy. Looking up, she sees a street-lamp's orange light plash across the grain and mottle of brickwork, and, above that, the full moon pushing through bone-thin cloud. Imagines she can hear its lunar tick.

'I feel fine, but I think I should go.'

'Well, if you're sure. Come back inside and I'll call a cab. There's a flat upstairs; you can wait there for it.'

She follows him up an iron staircase on the outside of the building, and through a door at the top. Once inside, he pushes through some large black felt curtains into a dark space filled with loud music and people dancing. She feels overwhelmed by the proximity of other bodies. He leans close to her and explains that they need to get to the other side of the room, then takes her by the hand and pushes slowly through the dancing crowd. When they are halfway across, the music changes and the crowd erupts with cheers as some old disco track Grace vaguely recognises begins to play. A young man grabs her free hand and starts moving her around, dancing with her, smiling and reaching for her other hand, and she reluctantly slides it from Luke's hold. In a sudden rush of euphoria, brought on by the drugs and the music and the mood in the room, she lets herself be swept away, dancing and smiling and watching him mouth the words, singing along to a chorus she's amazed to discover she remembers. When the song ends and a new one begins, the boy drifts away into the mass of bodies and she turns around to see Luke standing there smiling at her.

'Enjoying yourself?' he says.

'God, I haven't danced in years!' she says, exhilarated. 'I used to love dancing.'

On the other side of the dance floor, they emerge into an area with a bar and a queue for what she assumes must be the toilet. Luke waves to a girl behind the bar, who hands him a bottle of beer over the heads of those waiting to be served. He blows the girl a kiss before bounding up an uncarpeted wooden staircase. Grace follows. Upstairs, they enter a quiet lounge area, two sofas arranged around a low coffee table. The music's insistent thud vibrates the floor beneath their feet.

'Can I get you anything?' he says.

'I could murder a cup of tea,' she says.

'Coming right up,' he says, disappearing into the kitchen. She sits down in one of the sofas, comforted by its softness, feeling much better for being somewhere quiet. She feels strangely euphoric and eager to chat; wide awake and stupidly happy.

When he returns with the tea, she says, 'So who owns this place?'

He sits down on the other sofa and takes a swig of his beer. 'It's a squat, so no one owns it, or at least no one living here. There are about twelve here at the moment, I think. All artists. They throw amazing parties.'

'Honestly, I'm fine here on my own if you want to go and enjoy yourself,' she says, noticing his leg tapping to the music as it bleeds up through the floor.

'I am enjoying myself. I can dance later. Do you still want me to call you a cab?'

'I'm all right now, actually. I'm so sorry for over-reacting like that. I've never taken drugs before.'

'You ever taken Valium?'

'Yes.'

'Well, it's a bit like that, only better.'

'I do feel much better. Thanks for looking after me.'

'You didn't have that much. You'll be OK. If you want any more, just let me know.'

'God, no, I mustn't.'

His big green eyes sparkle with mischief, and she has the sudden, inappropriate urge to kiss him. Watching him run a quick hand through his hair, she recalls a night with Pete long ago, a fragment from that other life. The flotsam of another ocean.

THE TWO OF THEM had been lying on the sofa, enjoying a rare evening when they'd had her parents' house to themselves. And as he lay with his head in her lap, she began to comb out his quiff with her fingers and weave tiny plaits. When she'd finished she told him to look in the mirror, and he did, both of them laughing at the dainty, girlish plaits sprouting from his head, accentuating the prettiness of his face, making him look feminine, she thought, his eyes suddenly conscious of their coquettish width and beauty.

'YOU KNOW,' she says, 'you're a dead ringer for my first husband.'

'Really?'

'Here, take a look at this.' She removes her purse from her bag and hands him the photograph of Pete she'd found the other day. Stashing it there had made her feel slightly guilty, though now she feels no such emotion, only the quick, fierce need to be known.

'Wow! It really does look like me,' he says.

'I could've eaten him on a butty!' she says, and he laughs.

'Have you ever loved someone and it became yourself?'

'Yes,' he says. 'Do you mind if I photograph it?'

'Go ahead,' she says, watching him position the photo on the coffee table and take a picture with his mobile phone. 'He was a right bastard, though. Used to knock me around.'

'Shit. I'm sorry. It must have freaked you the fuck out when you first saw me.'

'Did it ever. Bloody hell...' *Brought it all flooding back, the fear and the love.*

Brought you here.

'I thought you were a ghost. Either that, or I was doolally tap.'

'I can imagine. But how do you get over a thing like that, losing someone you love?'

'You don't,' says Grace, 'not really. You just learn to live with it, which is a form of getting over it, I suppose.'

You hold it like a pebble, worrying it away but keeping it warm at the same time. You get to like the smooth shape of it in your hand. It begins to comfort you.

She tells him – she can't help herself – all about seeing him outside the shop, at the bus stop, the pub, and the ponds with Given. He looks down occasionally at the snapshot. When she's finished she feels panicky about divulging so much; cross with herself for blathering. 'I must sound like a stalker.'

Just then the door opens and Given enters, releasing into the room a short blast of music. 'There you are!' he says. 'I've been looking for you.' He sits down next to Luke and they exchange a kiss.

Grace's first instinct is to snatch the photograph up from the coffee table – for some reason she doesn't want Given to see it – but before she can retrieve it he's holding it up, saying, 'What's this? When was this taken?'

'It's not me, it's Grace's first husband.'

'Fuck! It's you, even down to the packet!' He looks at it a few more seconds, before passing it over to Grace's hovering hand.

'Lucky you,' he says as she snatches it. She wants to tear the thing to pieces now, but doesn't for fear they'd think her insane. Instead, she stuffs it shamefully into her bag, not even bothering to put it back in her purse.

Given removes a fold of paper from his pocket and unwraps it, tapping white powder on to a CD case lying on the table. 'Want a line, Grace?' he says and she declines. All these drugs, all these people on drugs, are making her anxious again.

'Where's Lind?' Luke asks. 'I thought she was with you.'

'I dunno,' Given says. 'I thought she was with you.'

'I haven't seen her since we got here.' Luke's thumbs drum his thighs.

'Don't you want to dance? The music's great.'

'Nah. Maybe later.'

Grace sips her tea, lights a cigarette, starting to feel an irrational and unspecified fear. The room seems to shudder, then settle. One look at Luke's face, though, and all thoughts of leaving dissolve. He gives her a big, generous smile, before springing to his feet.

'You OK here on your own while I go downstairs for a slash? I'll be right back,' he says, and is gone, in a flash. She looks at Given.

'I'm going to make another cuppa. Do you want one?'

'No, thanks.'

He's wary of her, she can tell, as she is of him. Her resistance to his charms is grating on him. He's unsure what to make of this strange old woman who's suddenly entered their lives. She stands and walks into the kitchen. As she's filling the kettle she notices a toilet there, just off the kitchen, and wonders if Luke knew that. Surely he knew that? By the time she's used it the kettle has boiled, and as she is filling the mug she spies a small bottle of whisky by the tea caddy. Pops a shot into her tea. When she re-enters the living room, Given is still there. She'd hoped he might have gone by now.

As she settles back into her seat, trying to think of something to say, he says, 'I fucking loved your comment earlier: "It's just wallpaper." You should be an art critic.' He laughs, and she isn't sure what to make of it. She lets the whisky warm her as she wonders how much longer Luke is going to be, annoyed with him again, this time for leaving her with this man she just wishes would go away. 'You don't like modern art much, do you, Grace?' he says.

She wants to reply that it's him, not modern art, that she doesn't like, but instead she says, 'I can't say I really understand it.' He laughs, and she adds, 'It's as if almost anything can be art if the artist says it is.'

'But for an artist that is totally liberating. It frees you up to do anything. Exhibit a urinal; cover an island in fabric. Or use your own body. Whatever.'

'I never thought of it that way.'

'So art becomes more of an attitude or way of being, a way of *seeing*, rather than a thing to be exhibited; a process, more than a product to be sold.'

'I'm a bit of a Philistine, I suppose.'

'So you live on a boat in the same marina as Luke and Linden?' It's a rather obvious change of subject but she is grateful.

'Yes. You own the boat they live on, don't you?'

'Yeah.'

'Have you seen what they've done to it?'

'No, but they told me about it. Sounds cool.'

'It's certainly very eye-catching! Though I think some of the other residents won't be sorry to see it go.'

'Linden tells me she's going to paint you,' he says.

'Yes. We've done the photos, but she hasn't had time to start the painting. You've kept her busy, I hear.'

'She's been a treasure getting the show.'

'I really like Linden,' she says.

'So do I,' he says, giving nothing away.

'How's it all going?' she says, fixing her eyes on him.

He nods slowly and says, 'It's going fine. You know – nothing serious.'

'Oh? I got the impression from her that it was.'

'It's early days, you know.'

She thinks she can see him start to squirm a bit, and in the grip of a sudden mischief she says, 'And what about Luke?'

'What about Luke?' He is losing the charm now; the mask is slipping, and she can see his eyes start to darken and steel.

'Well, doesn't he deserve to know?' she says, not nastily but firmly. 'They both do. I think it's wrong, what you're doing. You shouldn't play with people's emotions like that.'

'I think you should back off and mind your own business, Grace. It's got nothing to do with you. That's what I think.'

Day Seven

He stands up quickly and for the briefest second she thinks he is going to hit her, and she flinches.

'Don't look so scared,' he says. 'You can be pretty fearless when you want to be. I'm going to go and find Lind. See you later.' And he is gone.

Grace lights a cigarette and wills Luke to return. She could, she realises, be waiting hours. She considers going out to look for him, but feels too intimidated, too out of sync with her surroundings, and decides the best thing to do is stay put.

She stares at a large patch of yellow wallpaper on the wall opposite. She never saw a worse paper in her life. It is a smouldering, unclean yellow, with a recurrent spot where the pattern lolls like a broken neck and two bulbous eyes staring upside down. It has a kind of sub-pattern in a different shade; and she can make out a strange, provoking, formless sort of figure, which seems to skulk about behind the front design, like something viewed through the bars of a cage. The more she stares at it, the more she discerns that this figure is a woman, and that she is crawling around frantically, trying to escape from the pattern imprisoning her.

Grace thinks about the life she's leaving behind. This is all she can do, because to think about the future is to stare into an abyss. All those flat grey years after the breakdown, when her life became a box out of which she could not find her way, locked in a kind of numb grief that removed her from the world… The silence that grew between her and Gordon whenever they weren't either with the boys or discussing them. And, once Paul and Jason left home, the absence in her head of anything to say to him. The solitude, but also the relief as, increasingly, she spent nights alone in front of the television. His face whenever she mentioned Hannah; his incapacity or unwillingness to talk about her.

He belongs to another life now, a country to which she can't return. He is a ghost now too. She lets a deep, sad regret take hold, for the love that never grew. She can't imagine a future that would involve going back to him, but nor can she picture an alternative. She tries to conjure an image of what survival might look like, what form it might take, for her, here and now.

She stands and makes her way into the kitchen to hunt down something to eat. A packet of crisps only clarts up her already dry mouth and she has to rinse them down with water. The fridge offers up a raspberry yoghurt, and she makes short shrift of that, enjoying the moist, sweet gulps. She makes another cup of whiskytea before settling back on the sofa, wishing she had the courage to leave, feeling like a fool. Her bones ache with tiredness but her mind is whirring at a rate of knots, snapping like an angry dog, berating her for her stupidity, her brainless, idiotic stupidity. Telling Luke all that stuff, and then mouthing off at Given. It's Gordon's voice she hears, but it could just as well be her father's, or Pete's. *What were you thinking, woman?* The last word spat like an insult.

DAY EIGHT

AROUND THREE AM, Grace succumbs to tiredness, pulled into a deep unconsciousness, dreaming she's with Luke and Pete in a bedroom and they are kissing in front of her, ignoring her, or else not caring at all that she's there. And she can feel – almost as if it's real, she will recall later, the emotion remaining like a mood – a mixture of excitement and rejection, a sense of being excluded, together with the voyeuristic pleasure of watching the two men undress and start to fuck.

She drifts slowly awake to an insistent worm of music that has eaten its way into her dream. Opens her eyes to find the seats surrounding her occupied by half a dozen strangers. A young man next to her says, 'Hello,' and she croaks a reply, checking with a quick finger to her chin that she hasn't dribbled. Hopes she hadn't been snoring, or talking in her sleep. She asks for some water and he passes her a bottle from the table and she blushes as her head fills with the memory of the dream – the sight of Pete fucking Luke – or was it Luke fucking Pete? Identical bodies entwined, locked into and on to each other. She looks around at all the drug-bright young faces and feels as if she's just been exhumed. She asks the boy the time, taking in the tattoos – flowers and vines and leaves – sleeving his skinny arms. Buds and swallows. An anchor.

He says, 'It's half-five. Who did you come with?' and, when she tells him, a girl with red dreadlocks and a ring through her lip looks up from rolling a joint and says,

'I'm pretty sure they left a while ago. Do you have their numbers?'

'I think I'll just go.'

An open-mouthed yawn takes her by surprise, and she slaps a hand across her mouth and says, '*Excuse me.*' The boy offers to ring her a cab and she tells him where she needs to get to. She wants her bed and the comfort of its solitude. What the hell happened to Luke?

'I'll walk you out,' he says.

She says goodbye to the room and follows him down and outside into an early chill, and she shudders, pulling the pashmina around her. They walk through the tented forecourt, past sofas littered with sleeping bodies, the floor a storm of empty bottles and cans she's careful not to kick. Everything is silent now but for the ringing in her ears. Her mouth is pinched with dryness.

It is a cloudless blue-skied new day, and she remembers with a panic that she's supposed to leave for Manchester in a couple of hours. Before Gordon gets back. But all she wants to do is sleep.

As they're waiting for the cab, a green VW camper van pulls up with Luke in the driving seat.

'Grace, get in!' he shouts through the open window. 'I'll give you a lift.'

'No, it's OK, thanks, there's a cab coming,' she says, looking at the boy, avoiding Luke's gaze. She's hurt and angry with him for leaving her alone.

'It's all right,' the boy says, 'I can cancel it, or someone else can take it. It's not a problem.'

'Come on. Don't waste money on a cab.'

With a face like thunder, she climbs into the passenger seat and straps in. As Luke revs the van into motion she turns to wave but the boy has gone.

'Where the bloody hell have you been?' she says to Luke, 'leaving me sitting there like piffy on a rock bun.'

'I'm so sorry, Grace,' he says, and then she notices he's crying.

'What's wrong?'

'*Fucking Given!*'

'What happened?'

He smashes his fists against the steering wheel and lets out a yelp of pain.

'Look!' He turns to face her, revealing a right eye all bloody and swollen and a split lip. 'He fuckin' *hit me*!' The last two words come out in high-pitched disbelief.

'Bloody hell, are you all right?'

'No, I'm fucking not!' he says.

'Why did he do that?'

'I just asked him what was so wrong about people knowing about us. I said, "Are you ashamed or something?" – which really pissed him off. He said he wasn't ashamed, it just wasn't the right time. I asked when would be, and threatened to tell Linden right that second if he didn't; and then he *fucking lamped me*.'

'Dear God,' she says.

'Linden saw it all from across the room and came running over, and then all fucking hell broke loose.'

'Did he hit her?'

'No, but when she found out about me and him *she* hit him – right on the jaw!'

He lets out a laugh recalling it, and then winces with pain.

'She turned to me and said, "He's been fucking me, too, you know," and then stormed off. I've no idea where she is.'

'When did all this happen?'

'About an hour ago. I went back to the gallery to pick up the van and then I remembered you; came straight back. I'm so sorry.'

'Are you all right to drive?'

As he assures her he is, a police car passes in the opposite direction and Grace feels briefly anxious that they might get pulled over, though his driving is competent enough, she has to admit. Her heart keeps racing like a hamster in a wheel, edgy and fearful.

'Have you got any water?' she says.

'I haven't; here, have some of this,' he says, holding out a small carton of mango juice, a straw like an antenna. She sips.

'Christ! To think I thought I was in love with that sleazebag!' he says in a voice shrill with pain and incredulity. 'What a fucking twat!'

'I'm sorry, love,' she says, placing a quick hand on his knee.

'Could you light me a cigarette?' he says.

'Where did you get the van?' she asks, suddenly anxious it's stolen.

'It's mine. I used to live in it pretty much all the time before we moved on to the boat.'

'Were you homeless?'

'No, this was my home. *Is* my home.'

She hands him a lit cigarette and thinks about the day ahead. Should she try to get some sleep or head straight up to Jason's? She tries to remember where Gordon had said he was going, to work out how long it might take him to get back, only to realise he'd never actually mentioned where.

'I'm sorry, Grace. You must be furious with me.'

'I was when I woke up surrounded by strangers; I was embarrassed, and cross that you'd left me stranded. But I'm OK now. Thanks for coming back for me.'

She knows only too well how it feels to be assaulted by the one you love, and lets her fury go. How strange to see this image of Pete with a battered face. Almost redemptive.

'I had no idea he was fucking Linden as well,' he says, 'did you?' She isn't in the mood to talk but knows she can't very well ignore him.

'She told me the other night. I didn't know whether to tell you or not. It's none of my business, really, is it? I hardly know you.'

'No.'

'Besides, you both swore me to secrecy.'

They drive in silence through the waking streets as London, in a beatific light, sighs and receives the day. She doesn't want to get tangled in someone else's emotions, but she knows the only way to avoid that is to avoid other people all together; be entirely alone. And she doesn't want that, either. Not yet.

'Of course, it all makes perfect sense now,' he says, parking and switching off the engine, 'Why he didn't want her to know. He was telling her the same fucking thing. Two-faced prick!'

She notices the cuts on the knuckles of his left hand. 'I punched a wall,' he says, wincing as he flexes his fingers. 'Listen, is there any chance I can crash at yours? I don't wanna risk either of them coming back to the boat.'

'Of course you can.'

'I just need to stop off and pick up a few things.'

He reappears with a battered guitar case in one hand and the lace curtain in his other, like a jilted bride's veil. 'And I'm taking this back!' he says, jumping off the boat, and landing with a slight stagger. 'There's no fucking way he's having it now.' They make the short journey to her boat accompanied by birdsong and their own exhausted silence.

Day Eight

On the boat she cleans his face, thinking about the many times she'd done it to her own. The intimacy, the proximity move her; the shape of his lips moves her, the brightness in his eyes, the clarity of his skin; each curl of each eyelash stirs something. His face doesn't look so bad once the blood has been cleaned off, though the eye is swollen and bruised, and the lip is split. When their eyes lock, his gaze makes her melt into air. She feels a surge of love, all over again like the first time: the repetition of love like a memory replayed in all its furious glory. She knows it is hopeless, knows how it ends, but she can't seem to make it go away. 'See? I said you were Florence Nightingale,' he says when she's finished, and gives her a kiss on the cheek, making her blush. She is sixteen again, all bluster and ignorance, bold as a knife. A strange mixture of fear and desire takes hold as she turns and kisses him full on the mouth, holding his precious face in her hands, lost in knowing nothing at all. He gives a gentle push and the moment rips apart, revealing the here and now of her shame.

'I'm sorry,' she says, 'I don't know what – I can't imagine what I thought I was doing.'

'It's OK,' he says, at which point she bursts into tears, and he takes her in his arms. 'It's OK, it's OK,' he says.

When her tears subside, embarrassment sets in and she gently pushes him away. 'I'm so ashamed!' she says.

'Don't be. Honestly. Try and get some sleep.'

She goes into the bedroom and sits on the bed, pushes the shoes off her tired feet; unzips the dress and steps out of it; folds it and puts it in the open suitcase. Pulls her nightdress over her head and climbs beneath the duvet. She feels tired down to the bone but nowhere near sleepy. In the van she'd been practically sliding into a coma, but now she's in bed her mind is buzzing, her heart banging away in her chest. She can't stop visualising it getting bigger and bigger, imagining it bursting, like a blood-filled balloon, which only makes it beat faster. She tries to calm herself down with slow, shallow breathing, tries to empty out her mind; but it still keeps coming back to her: an unnamed guilt, a sense of having done something wrong, something irreparably grievous. She turns the pillow over and rests her hot cheek on the cool underbelly, wishing the fatigue in her bones would hush her frantic mind.

She can hear birdsong, and the windows are hung with pallid light, and from the other room the slow, sweet notes of Luke's guitar begin to flutter through like butterflies; followed by his voice, unexpectedly high and fragile. The words she is able to discern tell of the age-old tortures and woes of love, his angelic voice full of anger and heartache. Singing that man right out of his hair. The music fills the room, floating out upon the morning, over the rooftops, the curves of the river, losing itself in the silence of the upper air.

She dreams she is on a plane, crawling around on all fours, searching for her wedding ring. Frantically looking under seats, peeling back the carpet in her quest to find it. None of the other passengers takes any notice; it's as if she's invisible to them. And then she sees Gordon sitting at the back of the plane in his blue serge uniform, holding out his hand. She crawls over to him, and there in his palm is her wedding ring. Placing the ring in her mouth, he forces her to swallow it; he says, 'You're going nowhere, you cunt.'

She awakes with a choke to the sound of raised voices in the other room. Recognising Gordon's, she sits up, fighting for breath. Behind her eyes two dustbin lids clatter inside her echoing skull. The bedroom door flies open and Gordon enters, shouting, 'Grace, where are you? Who's that man out there?' His voice cuts through her head like a smoke alarm. 'What the hell's going on?' he says, his eyes wide with disbelief.

Grace climbs out of bed and reaches for her dressing gown. 'Nothing's *going on.*'

'Who's that man? And what have you done to your hair?'

'I fancied a change.'

'You look so different.'

'I *feel* different,' she says, thinking, *He must have noted Luke's resemblance to Pete; it can't have escaped him. It just can't.* It gives her a pleasurable thrill to have Gordon see Luke. *See, I'm not mad,* she wants to say. She walks past him and into the kitchen, wincing from the bite of the light. She greets Luke with a smile.

'Good morning, love.' The memory of the shameful kiss stabs at her insides.

'How are you feeling?' he says.

'Like I just got down off a cross,' she says, swallowing two painkillers. 'I see you've met Gordon. Don't be frightened, he's harmless enough.'

She raids her bag for cigarettes.

'Oh, that's right, go straight for the cancer sticks!' Gordon says.

'Fuck off, Gordon,' she says. She's never said that to anyone before. And it feels great. She wants to repeat it over and over into his face, into the face of the world.

'There's no need for that kind of language!'

'If I want to smoke I'll bloody well smoke,' she replies, emboldened by his shock, enjoying the feeling of liberation that comes with speaking her mind, accessing a rage she hadn't known was there.

'Why didn't you answer my calls? I rang a dozen times or more.'

She digs her mobile phone out of her bag, remembering she'd turned it off the night before. She switches it on. Ten missed calls.

'I was having a lie-in. It's not a crime.' She fills the kettle and switches it on, wondering where this fire inside her has come from. She notices her hands are shaking and feels charged with a fearful energy.

'But what's going on? Why is he here?' Gordon says.

'Nothing's going on! I didn't want to speak to you; I've nothing to say to you right now.' Looking down at a bowl of fruit that had looked fresh only yesterday, she notices the bananas have blackened and a green underbelly of mould is creeping from underneath the oranges. *Stick that in a gallery, call it* Neglect.

Luke stands up and says, 'Right, I need to hit the road. Grace, will you be OK?' She nods and watches him pick up the lace curtain and the guitar case and start heading for the door, to leave her with Gordon and her fury.

'Wait!' she says, and he stops, turning to look at her. 'Can I get a lift?'

'Sure.'

'Thanks. I'll meet you at the van in twenty minutes.'

'Cool,' he says. And then he is gone.

'Van? What van?' Gordon says, flustered, unsure how to act in the presence of this woman he barely recognises. He can see plainly that she is not herself. That is, he cannot see she is becoming herself, and daily casting aside that fictitious self that people assume like a garment in which to appear before the world.

'I'm leaving. I told you, I want a divorce.'

'But we have to talk about this! Where will you go?'

'I'll ring you in a few days.'

'I'm your husband and I demand to know where you're going with that man!'

She turns to face him. 'I'm going for a shower. Please be gone by the time I'm finished,' she says, walking over to the bathroom door. He follows her and she wonders briefly whether he will try and physically stop her leaving.

And how hard would she fight to get away?

'You can't just disappear with a total stranger without telling me where! For heaven's sake, woman, think about what you're doing! And what the hell happened to his face – has he been in a fight?' He's desperate again. She is about to close the bedroom door on him when he looks her in the eye and says, 'Why did you marry me, Grace? You didn't love me.'

'I did.'

'No, you didn't. Not really. Oh, you tried, I'll grant you that. I could see you trying your best.'

She says nothing, can say nothing, for he speaks the painful truth, the truth they have both spent their time together avoiding, and upon the denial of which they tried to secure some happiness.

'And that's OK, I gave up on you ever loving me a long time ago, but we get along, don't we? We muck along. What else are we going to do, at our age?' His voice is plaintive now. 'Don't go. Have a word with yourself. What on earth will you do if you leave? Where will you go?' He shakes his head. 'Who else will want you, at your age?'

'Goodbye, Gordon,' she says, closing the door on his baffled, frightened face.

Her whole body is straining to tremble. She just has to get away, and then everything will be all right. She needs to leave this life; it left her a long time ago. She removes her wedding ring and puts it inside her toiletries bag before stepping under the shower. *Is this what it amounts to?* she thinks as she dresses afterwards.

Two sons I never see and a husband who's a stranger?
There is an empty sorrow where her life should be. And
her life had fitted so neatly into one small case that it
makes her want to cry.

When she steps out of the bathroom, she's relieved to
see Gordon has gone.

In the bedroom, Hannah's diaries lie on the floor
beside the case. She doesn't want to take them, but nor
does she want to leave them for Gordon to read. He
doesn't even know they exist; they are hers, hers and
Hannah's. She carries them into the kitchen and over to
the empty sink. She tears out a page and holds the flame
of her lighter to the corner of it, then drops it into the
sink to watch it blacken and reduce. Page by page, she
destroys each book in turn, reducing them to a scatter
of ash.

She lights a cigarette from the last page before
dropping it, and it makes her remember someone she
hasn't thought about in years: one of the patients at
Parkside whom she befriended, a sixteen-year-old girl
who would set fire to her bed once a week. Each time, the
nurses would haul her off and confine her, but no sooner
was she back on the ward than she was starting another
fire. She said they locked her in one of the underground
cells everyone talked about with consummate fear,
though not all the patients believed her, as she was
the only one who claimed to have seen the cells. Grace
recalls how they'd all have to huddle in the clock tower
until the fire brigade had gone, every time Jane managed

to get her hands on a match. Watching the diaries turn to cinders, Grace finally understands why she did it: it feels good to watch things burn.

JANE ADMITTED to Grace that she started the fires because she liked it in solitary; it was the only place she felt safe. She said her parents had her put away because of her violent mood swings and inappropriate sexual behaviour. 'When they caught me getting something other than milk from the milkman it was the last straw,' she said. She was pretty and well-spoken, and flirted with any man who came near her.

Jane was the first person Grace spoke to, after that first week of not uttering a word. Grace sat next to her in the day room and said, 'There's been a terrible mistake and I shouldn't be in here at all.'

'Me too,' said the girl, scratching herself all over as if she had fleas.

'But I don't want to be among mad people,' Grace remarked.

'Oh, you can't help that,' said Jane; 'we're all mad here. I'm mad. You're mad.'

'How do you know I'm mad?' said Grace.

'You must be,' said Jane, 'or you wouldn't have come.'

Most of the time Jane was placid and sweet, and Grace enjoyed talking to her, but at other times a feral rage would ignite unexpectedly, and she'd attack anyone who came near: mad as the sea and wind when both contend which is the mightier. During one of these fits she walked up to Jane with open arms, slowly reassuring her she meant no harm and calming the girl down enough to let herself be embraced, until she was finally closing her arms around Grace, who held her while she cried, and five burly nurses stood there and watched. This crazy mad girl and this crazy mad woman sobbing embracing sharing a world of grief, Grace wishing the girl in her arms were Hannah, and dying a little because it wasn't; could never be.

And their gaolers looking on, devoid of all pity and fear.

REMEMBERING NOW, feeling once more the beat of the girl's heart against her, Grace knows, with a knowledge that somehow sets her free, all there is to know about life; which is, nothing. The vertigo of unknowing rushes through her.

When the flames die down she gives the ash a quick blast of the cold tap before collecting her case and locking the boat up for the last time. Pam appears and asks her if everything is OK; she couldn't help hearing raised voices earlier.

'It was Gordon. He came back early and we had a fight. I'm leaving him.'

'Fucking 'ell, Grace! I didn't see that coming.'

'Neither did he.'

'Have you got time for a coffee?'

'I haven't, love. I've got someone waiting.' Grace smiles when she realises how that must sound, and adds, 'It's not what you think. I'm not running off with another man. Well, I am, but it's far more complicated than that. I'll call you in a day or two and explain.'

As she approaches the van, the sight of Luke – looking at his phone and smoking – relaxes her a little; at least she won't be alone just yet. He opens the passenger door and says, 'Your carriage awaits,' taking her suitcase and stowing it inside. Out of nowhere, Gordon appears, begging her to come back to the boat so he can 'talk some sense' into her. 'I'm going to call the police,' he says, holding up his mobile phone. 'This is an abduction.'

'Go *away*, Gordon,' she says, climbing into the passenger seat, busying herself with the seatbelt to avoid looking at him. 'No one is being abducted.'

Luke shuts her door and walks around to the driver's side with Gordon at his heels, trying to assert an authority he no longer possesses, if he ever did. 'Where are you taking her? Where are you taking my wife? If you don't tell me, I'm going to report you to the police.'

Pedestrians stop and stare at the scene. Luke shuts the door and looks at Grace as Gordon taps on the glass, still shouting.

Vertiginous, she wavers. She could ask Luke to let her out; go back to everything; stay. Or she could go along. For the ride. She looks at Luke, at Pete's profile, trusting nothing but her own instinct to flee. This is the day, the moment; she feels nauseous. 'Just drive,' she says.

As they turn on to Warwick Avenue, he says, 'So that's Gordon!'

'I'm so sorry about that.'

'I thought for a second there he was going to punch me!'

She looks at his glorious profile.

'Gordon would never do that,' she says, adding, 'Pete would have, though.'

'So you're leaving him for good?' Luke says.

She pauses. 'What's that Liz Taylor film where she says to Paul Newman, "We don't live together, we just occupy the same cage"? It's been a bit like that with Gordon for a while now. But we were muddling along fine till I clapped eyes on you. Now my life feels like a jumper worn the wrong way around.'

'I'm sorry,' he says.

'Don't be; I'm not. All this is long overdue, believe you me. Have you ever daydreamed about just packing up and sodding off somewhere? Not telling anyone where you're going? Escaping your life. Starting again. That's how I feel. Like being someone else for a change.'

'I feel like that most of the time,' he says. 'Actually, *all* of the time.'

'I used to dream about running away to some small country village and working as a barmaid or a waitress or something like that.'

'Why didn't you?'

'The kids, I suppose. You can't do that when you've got a husband and kids, can you?'

'So do it now,' he says, making it seem so possible. 'I can understand why people go missing. That desire to remove yourself entirely. Absolutely fucking understand. Personally I'd like to fake my own death, because I do like to put on a show.'

They both laugh, breaking the tension. That he understands her and doesn't think she's gone completely off the rails relaxes her. She runs through all the people she knows, wondering if any of them would be so accepting of her walking out on her marriage like that.

'Do you still love him?' he says.

The question stumps her, but it has to be answered. For herself, more than anything.

'I don't think I was ever in love with him. Not like I was with Pete. Perhaps you only get to love like that once; I don't know. I've certainly never felt it again. But he's been a good provider, and I'm thankful for that.'

It's surreal to be talking about her feelings for Gordon with this replica of his nemesis – a betrayal and a liberation; necessary and uncalled-for. A luxury afforded.

Luke says, 'I can't imagine what it must be like to take those vows, to make that kind of commitment. I'm not sure I'd ever want to. And yet I'd love someone to ask me. How fucked up is that?'

'Be careful what you wish for,' she says, and he laughs, momentarily childish and bright.

'With Gordon, even on the actual wedding day I didn't feel excited at all. I remember thinking to myself as I walked down the aisle, *You shouldn't really be doing this, you know you don't love him*. Not the best way to start married life, is it?'

'So why *did* you marry him?'

'I thought I had to have a husband, and the kids a dad. It sounds mercenary, doesn't it, put like that? But I was more grateful than lovestruck, if I'm honest.' She lets out a quick laugh and says, 'He must have had a bloody shock seeing you there just now, in the flesh. He thought I was going mad, seeing ghosts.'

'I feel like a ghost,' he says. 'I feel like you could pass your hand straight through me.'

She taps a finger against his arm and says, 'No, you're real enough.'

'Sadly,' he says, and begins to cry.

'He's not worth your tears, love,' she says, patting his leg.

His mobile begins to ring. He presses 'end call' before throwing it over his shoulder, into the back of the van, where it lands on the bedding without a sound. 'So where do you want a lift to?' he says.

'I was going to stay with my youngest, Jason, in Macclesfield,' she says, 'but now I'm not sure. I don't want Gordon knowing where I am, and I think Jason would tell him. I don't want to see him for a while. But that's about all I do know right now.'

'Well, I've decided I need the healing power of the Highlands, so I can certainly give you a lift to Manchester if you'd like, or I can drop you off at Euston.'

'If it's no trouble, Manchester would be great.'

'No trouble at all.'

'I'll give you money for petrol. I'd have had to pay for a ticket anyway.'

Grace allows herself to relax a little, now that at least the next few hours of her future are accounted for. What she'll do in Manchester is anyone's guess. *When what you are doing is not what you want to be doing, what do you do?*

'I've never been to the Highlands,' she says. 'Always wanted to but never got around to it.'

'You'd love it,' he says. 'The remote wildness of the glens is just what I need right now.'

'Your dad lives in Scotland, doesn't he?'

Grace wonders how she would respond if he invited her to go there with him now.

'Yes – near Inverness. I'm thinking of calling in to visit. I haven't seen him since I told him I was gay five years ago and he threw me out of his house.'

'I wouldn't stop loving a child of mine for something like that,' she says.

'That's because you're a decent human being, while he's a homophobic arsehole. I decided then I never wanted to see the bastard ever again. But he rang me last week – first time in five years – to tell me he's got fucking lung cancer.'

'How far gone is it?'

'I don't know. He won't tell me. When I ask he says, "What do you care?" And we end up arguing until one of us hangs up. Usually me.'

'I'm sorry, love. And *do* you care?'

'Sure – he wasn't the greatest dad in the world but I love the old bastard. Anyway, I'll go and see him. Him and Mum haven't spoken in years so I'm really all the family he has left. He never remarried. Loves the bottle too much.'

They fall into silence again and she starts reading the road signs and shop-fronts to stop herself from thinking. *Won't someone please teach me how to be in this world?*

At a red light she stares into the window of a pet shop, reading a sign for a self-cleaning fish tank above a tank of dirty green water, brief flashes of orange appearing and disappearing against the filthy glass. At another red light they watch someone bellowing into a megaphone about how much Jesus loves everyone.

'*Bloody nutter*,' Luke says, and they laugh.

'Not the best advert for the church, is it?' she says.

'Or maybe it is.'

They stop at a garage in Chalk Farm to fill the tank. Grace pays for the petrol on her credit card, along with a litre bottle of water, two coffees, an egg and cress sandwich, and a packet of ready salted crisps for Luke. As they turn on to the A1, she says, 'When did you know you were gay?'

'I've always known. I was such a delicate, dreamy child. Always on my own, drawing or playing the guitar. And as far back as I can remember I've known I liked men rather than women when it came to sex. I started having sex with men at the age of fourteen. Came out when I was nineteen.'

'Have you ever slept with a woman?' she asks, surprised at how easily the question comes, and how readily he replies.

'Not since I was a teenager. I only really did it, I think, because I couldn't accept being gay. The world gives us a hard time sometimes, in case you hadn't noticed.'

'I didn't know what a homosexual was till I met Pete,' Grace says. 'We were in a pub one night on our honeymoon and these two fellas walked in wearing make-up and when I pointed them out Pete said, "They're queer." I didn't know what he meant and he had to explain.'

She asks about Given and he says, 'Lind and I met him at a party six months ago. The three of us instantly started hanging out together. He and I started fucking almost immediately, though I've no idea how long it's been going on with Linden. And I really don't feel like discussing it with either of them right now.'

'I'm sorry, love – would you rather not talk about it?' she says.

'I don't mind. Linden and I will be fine; I know we'll get through this. But I never want to see his face again.'

Her mobile starts to ring. Gordon. She puts the phone on mute and hurls it behind her, to join Luke's, and they both exchange a laughterful glance.

In the homogenised anonymity of a service station café, they sit down and eat. Or, rather Luke eats, tucking into a fry-up. Grace orders a baguette, but it's sharp as broken glass against the roof of her mouth so she leaves it. Instead she eats the biscuit perched on the side of her saucer, dunking it in her coffee first to soften it. Their silence is masked by muzak and the chatter and clatter of people. The harsh lighting illuminates the pale blue of their fatigue. Luke starts to cry quietly, and Grace wonders why it never gets any easier to watch a grown man cry. She recalls Jason's first teenage heartbreak. How she'd tried to comfort this six-foot giant of a young man sobbing like a little boy, knowing there was nothing she could do to remove the pain, not like when he was a kid with a scraped knee; a rub of Dettol and a kiss on the head and he'd be off out again. None of that with a broken heart. Always been too sensitive, that one, she thinks, whereas his brother is the complete opposite. Skin like a rhino.

'You must think I'm insane,' Luke says, wiping away his tears and laughing with embarrassment.

'I'm hardly in a position to judge,' she says. 'I was sectioned once.'

'Really?'

'In 1980 I had a breakdown. Gordon had me put away.'

And there it is, out in the open, for the first time since it happened.

'Why?'

'My daughter Hannah died of a drug overdose. It was exactly a year to the day since her death,' she says, recounting the events of that day up to reading the diaries: going to the grave, rushing back to start clearing her room. 'Gordon came home from work to find me naked in the front garden eating soil. I can't remember doing that. Blazed clean out of my wits, I was,' she says.

'What was it like?'

'Don't remember much, to be honest. I floated through the whole thing as if I wasn't there. So numb I couldn't even cry. I hadn't the wit or the will to live so I just submitted to it. Took every pill they handed me and lobotomised my grief.'

'And you're worried he'll do it again?' Luke says, rolling a cigarette now his food is finished.

'More worried *I'll* do it again.'

'You're the sanest person I know.'

'That's not saying much!'

They laugh again and the mood lightens. She is flushed and feels intoxicated with the sound of her own voice and the unaccustomed taste of candour. She's told someone and it hasn't destroyed her. Or him.

'It's not really that I'm worried he'd have me locked up again. It's just, whatever it was that was keeping me with him, it's run out. I've nothing left. I'd much rather be on my own.'

'It's a brave thing to be doing, at your age.'

'Bravery doesn't come into it, love. I've no choice,' she says, draining her coffee cup and standing up. 'I'm just going to use the loo. See you at the van.'

Day Eight

In the bathroom, she takes the photograph of Pete from her bag and tears it up into eighteen tiny pieces, flushing them away until nothing remains.

Stepping out into the sunlight, she feels lighter for knowing the photograph is no more, as if that black and white image contained all of her past and she is now finally rid of it. Wherever it was that she was going, she wouldn't be needing it. It didn't belong to her, but to another woman who no longer existed and yet who still breathed inside her. Destroying the picture has awoken a dormant self, bringing a courage she tries her best to own. The lost object is the one that never really goes away. She can hear Pete's voice in her head, saying, 'There is no love, there's only fucking.'

And it's OK for that love to endure, the way a splinter or a seed endure, despite all he did. But it's OK to be glad he's dead, too. Grace pauses and sniffs the air, taking a deep lungful before letting out a sigh. It is done. She's left him. She's left them both.

Luke asks if she can drive for a bit while he tries to sleep in the back. As soon as they're back on the M1, slow, thick tears start to run down her face. Her thoughts turn to the last time she saw Hannah alive. She'd been out shopping when she'd spotted her among a group of her friends, but Hannah had bolted before Grace could reach her. She hadn't been home for a month; not since the last time she'd been round demanding money. Grace had given her all she had and she'd left without saying a word.

Even before she died, Grace was grieving for her; had already lost her.

And the next time she'd seen her was in the morgue. Her chest tightens at the memory of the point when everything stopped making sense, the order of things upset entirely. When she'd locked herself inside a mood so dark she couldn't see her hand in front of her face.

Luke is not Pete, and Hannah is not Hannah, and I am not myself.

She still can't decide whether going to stay with Jason is the right thing to do. Will he try and talk her into going back? Will he tell Gordon where she is? How far would he collude in having her locked up again? The more she thinks about it, the more real her fear becomes. Can she trust him? Will she be safe there? Not knowing for certain saddens her. She is gripped by the fear that Gordon might even already be there when she arrives. If he went by train, she calculates, he'd easily get there before her. She pictures him standing there with two orderlies by his side, holding the straitjacket. It makes her feel sick. But, if she doesn't go to Jason's, where else? She regrets as never before losing touch with all her old friends. Knows she can't very well turn up unannounced after all this time. Or could she? *Hello. Remember me? Do you mind if I stay for a while?* She wonders how cheaply she can get a hotel room, realising she has no clue, it's been so long since she paid for one.

Increasingly, being alone right now seems her best option.

Day Eight

She's still crying as they approach Manchester. The sky has become an unbroken bank of pearly grey cloud from which a fine drizzle starts to fall. She switches on the windscreen wipers, thinking about the years she lived in this city, as a child and as a woman: a daughter, a friend, a mother, a wife. With these concepts a life is built; but where is home? Luke is fast asleep and she decides, on a whim, to make a small detour and drive past Parkside. Her heart is racing and her vision is blurry with tears.

ONCE INSIDE, Grace was ordered to strip and handed a white hospital gown and slippers. She was fed tranquillisers and ushered into a ward. The building was a riot of noise, night-time giving licence to cries and screams the daylight kept in check. One patient was slowly banging her head against the metal bed-frame. Several were keening or crying. One barked like a dog.

Grace lay in her bed, exhausted, defeated. Untethered. She could smell old urine mixed with misery, an outcast adult smell of those who had known and then been deprived of their knowing; the smell of stale polish and corners, and of doors that had been kicked and hammered upon for more than a century. She picked the soil from beneath her fingernails with her teeth, tasting the outside she feared she would never see again.

The next morning she was awoken by a nurse shouting for everyone to get up and slop out. She watched the other women file out of the dormitory, each clutching a slop bucket. Grace hadn't used hers, but she followed them anyway, to a large bathroom, where the pots were emptied into toilets with no doors on the cubicles. They were ordered back to the dorm to make their beds, and then fed more medication and taken to breakfast. After breakfast, all the cutlery had to be counted, a ritual, she discovered, that was practised after every meal.

'Come with me,' said one of the nurses. 'You're to see Dr Reubens now.'

Dr Reubens was gaunt and officious. The dark circles around his eyes told Grace everything she needed to know about his profession. He asked her to tell him what she remembered from the previous day. She told him she remembered everything up until the moment she had read Hannah's diaries; after that, everything was a blur. When he told her, she didn't believe him. Then the edge of a memory flickered; something she didn't want to accept was real, so like a dream had it appeared.

'Can I leave now?' she asked, after a timid silence 'I'm fine now. Really, I am.'

'We'd prefer to keep you here for a while, just to make sure.'

'But I want to go home; there's nothing wrong with me.'

'I'm afraid yesterday's behaviour would suggest otherwise. Mrs Wellbeck, things can go wrong with the mind just as they can with the body. The mind too needs to rest, sometimes – when it's broken, or has undergone some kind of trauma. Losing your daughter has been a terrible wound to your mental wellbeing. You need to rest. Then you can go home. You mustn't worry about anything while you're here. Just focus on getting well again. You'll be out in no time.'

After the consultation, a nurse walked her to the day room, where, high in one corner, a television poured noise into the silence. She looked around. A middle-aged man was staring out of the barred window, waving at nothing. A woman sat in one corner laughing quietly to herself. One woman called out bingo numbers – *Legs Eleven! Two Fat Ladies! Clickety Click!* – bursting into hysterical laughter at each one. Another counted the number of chairs in the room, over and over again, stopping when she lost count and starting again. Grace took a seat as far away from everyone as she could and stared at the backs of her hands, wondering how long she'd have to stay.

It was a week before she uttered a word to anybody. The nurses never required you to say anything, and if another patient spoke to her she would ignore them. Walk away, if necessary. During those first seven days she tried to remain as inconspicuous as possible. She submitted, entirely, to the foggy routines of the hospital, feeling suddenly free of all worry; feeling cared for. She watched and tried to take the measure of the people around her, both patients and staff; tried to figure out the workings of this new reality. The hierarchy among the patients favoured obedience, while the hierarchy of the staff favoured power. The only logic to the meting out of punishment seemed to be based on personality, or perhaps mood. The slightest disobedience could result in a physically violent penalty from some nurses, while others might only issue a verbal reprimand; a small minority would even treat the patients with kindness. If you 'behaved', you avoided punishment. Grace knew from what she saw that her best option for getting out was to assume absolute docility. She was good at that.

During the six weeks she spent at Parkside, Grace was not punished even once, for she never disobeyed. Everything that was asked of her, she did: make the bed, *take this pill*, have a bath, eat this; mop the endless corridors; clean the toilets, *take this pill*. Sit there and do some basket-weaving. Eat this. *Take this pill*. Sleep. She succumbed to the pallid security of her days. After all, hadn't she abnegated her will long ago, when a ring was placed on a finger, or a baby in her arms? She saw the other patients get beaten for acting or speaking out of turn; saw their personalities burnt away with ECT, their wills removed with a scalpel. The part of them that didn't conform lopped off and thrown away. She took the path of least resistance in order to survive and escape.

Gordon didn't visit her once; nor did the boys. She would get angry about that, and then thank her lucky stars she didn't have to see him. She had wrapped a cocoon of silence around her as a buffer against the outside world, and for now that was all she needed.

Her mother came only once, after she'd been there five weeks, to tell Grace to pull herself together and get back to looking after her family. 'They need you. Think of them. Of your duty to them.' *What about my duty to me?* she wanted to say, longing for her mother to leave and let her return to her shell.

After the assessment period – during which she never saw Dr Reubens again, nor any other doctor – she was released, just in time for Christmas. When she stepped into the house she felt as if she was greeting strangers. She could see it in their eyes: fear. Paul and Jason were at that age when boys ceased showing much affection to their mothers, but even Gordon simply said hello and gestured to her seat in the corner of the living room. No kiss or hug. She sat down, feeling their discomfort; feeling unclean. Feeling a huge gulf appear between her and everyone else she knew. She'd seen things they hadn't seen; witnessed the lives of 'those mad people'; been one of them, for a while. Not as lost as some, perhaps – she'd never tried to kill herself or imagined she was made out of glass; never accused the kitchen of cooking the patients one by one. But she had a knowledge now about life on this planet that her friends and family lacked, and it set her apart. She knew what happened to the people who couldn't cope; knew where they ended up and how they were treated. How long would she feel on the wrong side, an impersonator of her own life, forever striving to keep at bay what she feared was only a scratch away?

AS SHE PULLS UP outside the old hospital – now converted into residential buildings – Grace stops crying. Even in this Gothic twilight it is no longer the forbidding Hammer Horror mansion of her memories. She considers getting out but the rain decides her against it. The clock tower she remembers as a bleak prison of tortured souls looks inert and inept, hopelessly innocent. The whole place now strikes her as soulless.

Luke's voice comes through the dark. 'Where are we?'

'Go back to sleep, love, we're not there yet.'

She turns the key in the ignition and releases the clutch, feeling more aware of her senses, more in the world and of the world than ever before; more alive. Yet this in itself, this feeling more alive, creates as much anxiety as joy, for along with it comes the inevitable blast of mortality, of living a life that must end, that could end right here, right now. When she parks outside Jason's she still hasn't decided if she'll even ring the bell. She wakes Luke.

'I'm getting out here,' she says.

On the pavement, Luke puts down her suitcase and retrieves her mobile phone from where she'd thrown it earlier. They exchange numbers and make promises to keep in touch, and he offers to pick her up on his way back to London. They embrace, and she knows she'll probably never see him again. But that's OK. She doesn't know where she will go now, but she knows it's time, finally, to be alone.

She stands outside the gate leading to Jason's front garden, watching the van drive off. Once it's out of sight, she turns and walks away. The city, and beyond that the world, is crying out for attention. She can do nothing for anybody any more, thank God. This is how to disappear completely: putting one foot in front of the other down that lamplit street, or down to the beach, where the children loved to play in the warm clear ocean once the sun began to set and the moon to rise. As she drops her mobile phone into the nearest bin, thinking about how unhappy she's been, and for how long, she knows her crushing need to be sheltered has disappeared. Like a ghost when the lights go on.

Author's note

Parts of this novel are inspired by the following:

Samuel Beckett, *Murphy*
Lewis Carroll, *Alice's Adventures in Wonderland*
Kate Chopin, *The Awakening*
Janet Frame, *Faces in the Water*
Marge Piercy, *Woman On The Edge of Time*
Charlotte Perkins Gilman, 'The Yellow Wallpaper'
Sylvia Plath, 'Parliament Hill Fields'
Jean Rhys, *Voyage in the Dark*
Elizabeth Smart, *The Assumption of the Rogues and Rascals*
Virginia Woolf, *Mrs Dalloway*

Acknowledgements

Firstly, I'd like to thank my parents, Jean and Philip, whose generosity and support has not only made this novel possible, but has also made me the person I am today.

I am forever indebted to the staff at Myriad. For editorial assistance offered with infinite patience, thank you Candida Lacey, Holly Ainley and Vicky Blunden. We got there in the end! For the most expert copy-editing a writer could wish for, thank you Linda McQueen. Thanks also to Corinne Pearlman, and my agent, Adrian Weston. Finally, thanks to all my friends and family for keeping my spirit alive.

Read on for an extract from Jonathan Kemp's
critically acclaimed debut novel *London Triptych*:

WINNER | Authors' Club Best First Novel Award

WINNER | QRG Best Book Award (Fiction)

SHORTLISTED | Green Carnation Prize

SHORTLISTED | Polari First Book Prize

1954

Another arrest reported in the papers this morning. Some poor sod caught in a public toilet. Hardly a week goes by without one. Now, I can't claim to know much about it, but it seems to me that when old men hang around public toilets while younger men are pissing, we aren't out for a glimpse of cock, or even a grope. No, in truth what roots us to the spot is the most profound feeling of envy because we can't piss like that any more. Respect, even. When you reach fifty, it trickles out.

He pisses like a horse. I can hear him through the whole house. A veritable Niagara. It's not a big house – he calls it 'the doll's house', to my chagrin. Tall as he is, he's forever banging his head on my lampshades and doorjambs, as I totter behind him. He strides through my tiny rooms with such confidence and familiarity, as if it were a castle and he its prince, and I feel like the valet who can call nothing here my own.

He has so much life in him that it's made me realise for the first time that I am old. And it's not a feeling I'm happy with. Not at all. It's not something I ruminated on and came to a calm decision about. Not something I've been refusing to accept and can no longer hold in abeyance. I simply looked at my face in the mirror and said aloud, 'You are old.' It's not even the exterior that made me gasp with horror – the grey hair, the lined face, the tarnished eyes.

These things I know. I see them every day. I can live with looking old, just about. Or at least I could, until recently. But I have met a boy whose youth makes me feel ancient to the very core, ossified and pointless. That's what made me smart.

When I first saw him, a month or so ago, I thought him quite the handsomest boy I'd seen in a long time. He wears his hair slicked into a quiff, and sports the general attire of what a newspaper last year nicknamed Teddy Boys. But when he removed his clothing I realised for the first time what I'd been missing in a model: someone who shines more when they are nude than when clothed. Skin with light trapped beneath it. Skin that looks complete, rather than exposed; that looks painted, full of colour and life, blood blue and flesh pink. Yellows, purples, whites. Tints I don't know I could ever reproduce. Strangely, he seems more relaxed when naked, more himself, more at home in his flesh than in his clothes. And because of that you don't really notice that he is naked.

His body is not exceptional, but he has tremendous definition, and a masculine grace that is best expressed by the word 'noble', if that doesn't sound too grand. When he speaks, however, it is with the jagged edges of simplicity. And, while that is not without its charm, it is clear that the sophistication of his being is concentrated on the surface. All his grace lies there, beautiful and richly visible. Within is merely an embryonic soul, his speech suggesting nothing but the workings of a half-grown heart.

In the presence of such concentrated beauty, I feel inspired for the first time in aeons: inspired to capture it in all its complexity and texture, all its pale beauty. I fill acres of paper with his crouched figure, his legs bent and twisted beyond recognition, his spine an abacus, a string of pearls arching impossibly as he nearly swallows himself like Ouroboros. The damp, dark caves of his armpits. The hairless plateau of his belly, tight and contoured. The planed edges of his muscular buttocks, carved to Hellenic perfection. If I placed my tongue there, I should expect them to be cold and hard as marble. The masculine sweep from his hairline to the right angle of his shoulder as fluid and mesmerising as any waterfall; the line of gravity that runs the length of his torso, from the hollow of his throat to the jewel of his navel, cruciformed by the stigmata of his nut-brown nipples blurred with hair; the pucker of his anus like a knot in a tree.

I can't help but wonder what it must feel like to be so exposed to the gaze of another, to know that you are being stared at and scrutinised. We seem to be obsessed with doing everything in our power to deny or avoid the thorny question of the body unclothed, except perhaps in art. All we have now is shame, and fig leaves, and sniggering like schoolgirls. All we have is prudery. How then does this young man feel, spread out before me? How can he not feel shame? I wonder.

After he left today, I walked into the bathroom and looked at myself in the mirror, and it was then that I muttered like an incantation the words, *You are old*, the second-person address granting a distance that in no way diminished the painful truth. His presence diminishes me. And it is more than feeling too old to interest him sexually, and more than wanting my own youth back again: I am racked with envy that I am not him. They say desire and identification are almost indistinguishable, but I never understood it till I saw him in all his luminescence – a thing I have certainly never possessed. I removed my clothes and stood naked before the mirror, something I haven't done for at least forty years. It shocked me, suddenly, to reflect that at no point in my life, beyond that curiosity which adolescence precipitates, have I paid any attention to my body. I looked at my reflection, at my rounded, narrow shoulders with their tufts of grey hair, my rotund belly, my shrivelled privates, my stick-white legs, and I felt nothing but a deep, vertiginous sadness.

There comes a time in life when youth becomes just a word; a word whose meaning you almost feel impelled to look up in a dictionary, so strangely does it sit upon the tongue. I think it was Oscar Wilde – or was it George Bernard Shaw? – who said that youth is wasted on the young. And he was right. You look back on your own youth and view it with the eyes of another person, and it seems as foreign as another country, as distant as a star.

But sometimes, if you are lucky, you are allowed to view another's youth up close and scrutinise the glory and the invincibility of that infallible state. Perhaps that is why people have children. And, by the same token, that must be why childless old men like myself feel it all the more brutally, and crave it in others. I cannot now recall what it felt like to be young. I suppose that is because I was too busy *being* young to think about it. Or perhaps because my youth does not in truth warrant recollection. But I must have been a youth, at some stage in my life, all things considered! Must have been in some sense flawless and innocent – but again these are words whose definition evades me. Photographs must supply some clue. Almost another face entirely stares back at me though, from the few I do possess, never having liked to have my picture taken. I see in them a stranger, whose ways and wiles I no longer recollect; whose passions and fears are irretrievable now.

Christ, and I'm only fifty-four.

This young man has awoken me not to the value of my own youth, but to its tarnished loss and frivolous and unforgivable waste. He is a free spirit, as free a spirit as I have ever known, whereas I have never felt free. So, while his presence is a source of joy, it is also a source of incredible pain, throwing into stark relief the woeful inadequacies of my life.

1998

This night is the place from which I must move forward. I'm to be released tomorrow and resume my life, yet there are so many questions crowding my thoughts as I recall the events that led me here. When I walk out of here tomorrow morning, I would like to feel I'd left it all behind, but I brought it all in here with me and I'll take it with me when I go. The past has a crushing substance. I'm on a tightrope, high above the ground, assailed by fear and panic, no safety net beneath me. I daren't look down and I daren't look back. I don't know what tomorrow looks like. But I need to try, at least, to understand. I need you, of all people, to understand me. It's because of you, after all, that I ended up in prison. But one of the many lessons I learnt in here is that things are what they are and will be what they will be.

This is for you, Jake. I never told you much about my past during the brief time I knew you. One of the great things about our time together is how in-the-moment it all was, how little we actually shared about our lives outside of the here and now of our bodies together. Not that we didn't speak, but somehow our childhoods, our pasts, never surfaced much as a topic of conversation. I've tried my best to erase mine, and not to have to speak of it to you was something I cherished. So this is for you, whether you read these words or not.

It's for me too, of course, though for completely different reasons.

As children, my elder brother and I, together with a group of other kids, would play on a nearby railway track, by a tunnel through which goods trains would occasionally pass – great rusting hulks of metal following one another in single file. We played chicken, standing on the tracks for as long as we dared as the train hurtled towards us. I always won, was always the last one standing there as the train rammed its way nearer. Every time, the others would flee to the sides of the track, leaving me alone, my heart racing. I can still remember watching the front of the train darken as it passed from sunlight into the black mouth of the tunnel. Only then would I run to the sidings. This wasn't an act of bravery. It took no courage on my part, because I didn't care that the train might pulverise me. I just wanted the rush that came from imagining my flesh spread across the front of that train. Even then, at that age, I used danger as a way of escaping boredom.

Growing up, I wanted for nothing. I had any toy I desired. I had affection, security, I never went hungry, my parents never missed a birthday, never neglected or beat me. In fact, they gave every sign of loving me – or if they didn't love me they certainly knew their duty and performed it well. They were good parents, and I was a good boy, an angel – never getting into trouble, never offending, always polite. Not because I wanted to be good, particularly, but because it was easier than doing anything else. Nothing existed for me – nothing real anyway. Fuelled by television, books and, most importantly, music, I constructed another place, a place I could value. In that tiny village I was cursed to endure, life was a thing with no value. The people around me seemed to live their lives like a person with one foot nailed to the floor, inscribing a perfect circle in the rotten earth and calling it home. Not only were the houses where we lived semi-detached, so were most of the lives. I longed to escape.

The lights have just been put out. I can hear my cellmate, Tony, beneath me, beginning to snore as he slides into sleep. Before long he'll be snoring louder than a sow in labour, and I envy him that sweet release into oblivion. He's from Hornchurch. In for stealing a car. He's not been here long and no real friendship has developed between us. I've struggled to find some common ground but every conversation gets beached by our differences, and our inability to communicate. I'll probably never see him again. And I probably won't sleep tonight. Too many memories crowding in, vying for attention.

As if that ever did any good, raking over the past.

Because I'd spent my childhood doing more or less exactly as I was told, it was assumed that I would continue to do so. On the night before I had to confirm my O-level options, my father mapped out the entire geography of my future. I was told what I would do with the rest of my life. And the flatness of the terrain he described made me despair. He wanted me to have a secure future. He wanted me to become an accountant, or at least 'in business' at some level. Something secure, something steady and lucrative. My father, who was a bank manager, not just by profession but also by nature, spoke to me that night as if he were turning me down for a loan. The subjects I loved – art and English literature – were not considered at all, while the subjects I hated – mathematics and economics, physics and chemistry – were attached to me like shackles. I nodded as he spoke, and the narrowness of my future oppressed me.

When my father was a baby, his mother taped his ears back onto his head while he slept in his cot, in order to prevent them folding forward and sticking out permanently. Sometimes, it seemed to me as if that tape had never been removed, and it prevented him from hearing anything I said. Each morning the same routine: he'd slice twenty discs of banana onto his cereal, and if, after twenty, he had a stump of fruit left, he would look up forlornly, unsure what to do with the excess. My mother would hold out her hand for him to drop it into her cupped palm. If he were ever to articulate what he feels about life, I'm certain he would claim that habit is the only route to happiness, or at least success.

My mother, in her own way, was equally taped down. Her overwhelming desire for an easy life rendered her incapable of contradicting anything he said. A more repressed human being I've yet to meet. She died three months after I was sent here. Cancer. I still haven't cried about it. I've cried about lots of things, myself mostly, but not her. I've had one visitor. An old client, now more of a friend – Gregory. Over the past year or so he's come here regularly, almost like my confessor. I told him I hadn't kept in touch with my family at all, and he said I should write. I did, knowing they wouldn't have moved address since I left. The first letter from my father told me about my mother.

It didn't occur to me at the time that I had any other option than to accept – or at least to give the appearance of accepting – their terms. From that point until I completed my O-levels two years later, I began a life of duplicity in order to survive. Lies became my way of cheating boredom, the portal I would crawl through to reach a world in which I could breathe.

To the outside world – and, most importantly, to my parents – I was the perfect scholar. Though I hated the subjects they foisted upon me, I knew the secret to an easy life lay in doing well at school, for the time being at least. So I spent my days studying maths and economics, and I spent my nights with my friends – and they were not the sort of people of whom my parents would have approved. A schoolfriend of mine, Phil, was working at the time in a small bistro in a posh part of town, washing dishes from seven till midnight, seven nights a week. Under the pretext of working there I was able to stay out every night till late. Dad liked the idea that I was willing to work. In reality, far from spending my time elbow-deep in boiling suds and grease, I cycled each night to the local golf course, to meet a crowd with whom I could smoke and drink myself into oblivion. There was Spike, with his skinhead and boxer's brawn, whose stepfather was forever in and out of prison and whose mother was too pissed to care what he got up to. Sometimes he would steal a car and drive us up to Saddleworth Moor. He was related to one of the victims of the murders that had taken place in the city in the mid-'60s, and he would take us to the spot he claimed the dead girl had been buried. Johnny, Spike's cousin, had long hair and wore AC/DC T-shirts. His elder brother was a dealer and he always had what seemed like an endless supply of dope and acid. The lights of the city hummed the colour of radioactivity as we drove back home. Heather, Johnny's girlfriend, was all shaggy hair and denim. They both head-banged along to the loud rock music that was played in the car. But Julie was my favourite. Julie never head-banged. Julie looked like Marilyn Monroe, or so we thought. She confided in me once that she was actually trying her best to look like *Mike* Monroe, from Hanoi Rocks, but no one seemed to care much. She wore her hair impeccably bleached and her skirts explicitly short, and was known as the village bike because she let most boys do pretty much anything with her. Most of the time, though, she was Spike's girlfriend.

I thought that only drugs or music could supply me with the transgressive thrill I sought. I never gave sex much thought. I had had a lacklustre and lustless grope with Julie one night before she and Spike started what my grandmother would quaintly call 'courting', but on the whole I knew even then that I preferred boys – knew that I would rather be kissing Spike. I hid this desire beneath a smog of drugs, claiming a cynical lack of interest in anything sexual, even though I imagined Spike naked and tied to my bed each time I masturbated. Spike and the others mockingly called me the Poet because books and the lyrics to songs – and the thoughts they inspired – were more important to me than trying to get laid. Whenever we got stoned they would all sink into torpor around me while I grew more and more animated by my own fucked-up monologue, till one of them would shout, 'Hey, Poet, fuckin' *can* it, will ya?'

Then I discovered whoring.

I wanted more than anything to leave this world behind, but not in order to destroy myself; only in order to find another world, one in which bodies glowed and danced like flames. Such a world is not found, however, but must be created anew each time we want to live in it. I know that much at least.

1894

The name's Jack Rose, or *Rosy Jack* as the gents like to call me, on account of that soft pink bud nestling between me rosy arse cheeks. I'm a Maryanne, see, and gentlemen pays me handsomely to do things I should likely enough do for free, though the cash definitely helps, make no mistake. Steamers, we call 'em, the gents what come around; or swells or swanks: moneyed geezers, well-mannered, classy, not like the lowlife I knew before I started in this game. But they all, to a man, love that arse of mine, love watching it pucker and pout, the filthy bastards – love to poke it, finger it, sniff it, lick it, fill it, fuck it. And I love them to do it, I'm not ashamed to admit. But I love too the gifts and cash what they show their appreciation of my little rosy star with – my asterisk of flesh, my puckered pal. This hole of mine has turned out to be a right little golden goose.

I don't suppose boys are any different from girls in liking to take presents from those what are fond of us. There isn't much wrong in gents showing their appreciation of the finer things in life with a trinket or a few shillings, is there now? I wasn't the first and I doubt very much I'll be the last, that much I do know. I know too that it is a harsh world, and harder still in this bloody shithole city of London I was pushed into. Fuckin' impossible if the jaws of poverty hold you as they hold me ma and pa and the other seven miserable brats he sired. If that's your lot you'd do well to keep your eyes shut and crawl right back into the cunt you came from, if only that was an option. Instead we open our eyes and crawl forward, lambs to the slaughter every last one of us. A smack on the arse and you've no bloody choice is the truth of the matter. Every day a fuckin' battle. So if you can claw back a little happiness, a little pleasure, a little laughter and joy, it's no crime. It'll come as no surprise then when I confess that I feel like the king of the world when a coin is pressed into my palm after being pleasured. It's bleedin' hilarious to be making money so easily, isn't it? And this line of work takes me places I'd never have seen otherwise, that's for sure. When you have nothing to begin with you only stand to gain, and the way of life most rich gents take for granted seems to me to be the trappings of heaven itself. And the police are kind to me after their fashion. They shut their eyes for the most part – but then they've shut their eyes to worse than me and no mistake. The things I've seen in this town would make even old Queen Vic crack a smile.

Odd the way I fell into the whole business, really. By accident, you might say. I certainly never planned it, but then again I don't suppose anyone ever sets out to become a whore, do they? It was a bollock-numbing January in '93 and I was several months past my fifteenth birthday, though I looked much younger. Skinny as a runt and no trace of a beard as yet, though I had sprouted a soft dark down on my privates which thrilled me. I was running telegrams. Fuckin' awful, it was. Perhaps you've known it yourself, that horror when you realise all your time is being given over to others, all your thoughts are about day-to-day survival. Perhaps like me you've felt yourself chained to a fate you detest. I don't know. Where I grew up, ugliness was the one and only reality; joy was unheard of except for the odd booze-up or street fight. I was working about fifteen hours a day running around in all weathers.

I was born and raised in Bethnal Green, a stinkin' hole of a place with a cesspit the size of a small lake down the road from our home that filled the air with the stench of shit the whole time. We shared the house with three other families. We had no running water so going for a piss or a crap meant finding a space that hadn't already been used – in or outside the house. We were all of us permanently sick and two of my sisters died before even learning to walk. My pa is a useless alcoholic crook. Never done a day's work in his life. Robs to get his beer money and we never saw a penny of it. He's violent and spiteful, too, to all of us. One day I came home to find my two little sisters, Millie and Flossie, crying something awful, and, when I could finally get some sense out of them, it seems Pa'd got them to pull on a piece of string threaded through a keyhole in the front door. 'Pull it hard, girls,' he'd said, so they did, eager to please their pa, not knowing that on the other side of the door the string was tied around the neck of a stray cat. He swung the door open to show them the poor strangled beast hanging there, dead by their own fair hands. That amused him no end. The cunt.

He beats Ma all the time. She always puts up a fight but she always comes off worst, poor cow. He's a big fucker. I got good at cleaning her up afterwards. We were scared shitless, the little ones crying and screaming every time he was around. I'll never understand why Ma married him in the first place. I asked her once and all she said was, 'He used to treat me like gold.' Sure, it's good to be treated like gold, but I can hardly believe that ole bastard even knows how. She's deaf in one ear after he thought it a lark to smash two cupboard doors closed on her head one day.

It was all Ma could do to feed us proper once a week, let alone once a day. Then at the age of fourteen a stroke of luck landed me a job as a messenger for the Post Office in Charing Cross. True, I was delivering grams in storm and snow, frozen to the bone, miserable as sin and tired as a dog. But being a thick bastard I considered myself fuckin' lucky. All my friends, my elder brothers too, had turned to crime, for where we lived it was steal or starve. I come from a fine line of criminals – though not very good ones. Pa was always behind bars. If we ever needed to find him, we knew he'd be in the pub or in the clink. But for some reason I couldn't bring myself to do it. My one and only joy was handing my wages to Ma once a week and seeing her face light up from the glow of the coins, both of us knowing I'd earned them honestly. But I was soon to discover another much greater source of both money and pleasure, a way of life that would show me things beyond that narrow horizon of poverty and survival.

Strangely enough, I never thought it a crime, becoming a renter.

MORE FROM MYRIAD

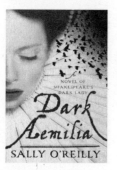

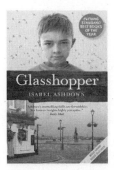

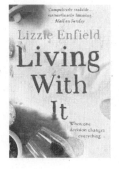

MORE FROM MYRIAD

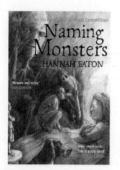

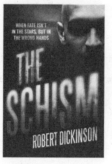

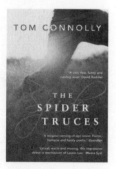

Sign up to our mailing list at
www.myriadeditions.com
Follow us on Facebook and Twitter

Jonathan Kemp was born in Manchester. He now lives in London, where he teaches creative writing, literature and queer theory at Birkbeck, University of London. His debut novel, *London Triptych*, won the Authors' Club Best First Novel Award. He is also the author of *Twentysix*.